Mike & Patty
Love You Guys
Mike

The Magic Book

Mike Holst

iUniverse, Inc.
New York Bloomington

The Magic Book

Copyright © 2009 by Mike Holst

All rights reserved. No part of this book may be used or reproduced by any means, graphic, electronic, or mechanical, including photocopying, recording, taping or by any information storage retrieval system without the written permission of the publisher except in the case of brief quotations embodied in critical articles and reviews.

This is a work of fiction. All of the characters, names, incidents, organizations, and dialogue in this novel are either the products of the author's imagination or are used fictitiously.

iUniverse books may be ordered through booksellers or by contacting:

iUniverse
1663 Liberty Drive
Bloomington, IN 47403
www.iuniverse.com
1-800-Authors (1-800-288-4677)

Because of the dynamic nature of the Internet, any Web addresses or links contained in this book may have changed since publication and may no longer be valid. The views expressed in this work are solely those of the author and do not necessarily reflect the views of the publisher, and the publisher hereby disclaims any responsibility for them.

ISBN: 978-1-4401-8656-1 (sc)
ISBN: 978-1-4401-8657-8 (ebk)

Printed in the United States of America

iUniverse rev. date: 11/05/2009

Also by Mike Holst

A Long Way Back
Nothing to Lose
No Clues in the Ashes
Justice For Adam

This book is dedicated to all the keepers of the books, wherever they may be.
A special thanks once more to Kitty, for all of her help and encouragement.

Prologue

On a dark and dusty book shelf, in a long forgotten bookstore in downtown St. Paul, Minnesota, there laid an old nondescript manuscript. Yellowed with age and long forgotten, it lay there in waiting for a chance to tell its story.

Had overly shy, young Jennifer Crawford known what supernatural things would happen when she started reading that story, she never would have opened it. But she did, and she was taken on a strange and bizarre journey to another time and another place. It wasn't the place, the time, or the journey, that was so strange. It was her involvement in it, and the part she seemed to willingly play in the story that was so troubling.

So come along with Jenny on a literary trip, to a time and a place and a world almost forgotten. A rendezvous with a mysterious man, she never knew-- or did she? Was he real, or was he somehow born from the depths of her subconscious mind.

ANOTHER DAY, ANOTHER TIME

CHAPTER ONE

Jennifer Crawford had never entertained a thought about owning a bookstore. She hadn't ever worked in a bookstore, or hardly ever patronized one. That was because she worked in a small library on the campus of St. Theresa's college in southern Minnesota and was generously surrounded by books all of the time.

Jenny loved books and she was an avid reader. Books and stories took her out of her mundane, sheltered life style and gave her the opportunity to travel many places she had never been, and gave her a chance to take on roles in her imaginational journeys she had never thought possible. From the time she was a little girl back in St. Paul, Minnesota, her toys lay nearly untouched, but her books were always on her bed. Many of them were worn out by her constant attention and she knew most of them from cover to cover, by heart.

In school in her elementary years she was an A+ student and the smartest kid in her class. Not because she had such a high I.Q.-- far from it. It was her constant thirst for knowledge and the books she almost worshiped that made her so smart. She had started on one end of the tiny school library and worked her way up and down and across the shelves, always looking for more information and more stories. By the time she entered high school she had read almost every book in the library.

When birthdays and Christmas came along and her father asked her what she wanted, she would always give him the name of another book, and soon her room and their house was inundated with a plethora of books. Her bewildered father, who rarely read anything more then the daily newspaper, could only shake his head, but deep down he was proud of his little bookworm. After all she was all he had. His wife had died in childbirth and he had never found another woman that he could, or would, trust with his beloved Jenny.

In high school the saga with her reading continued. The physical and emotional changes that come to most girls her age had arrived, but Jennifer had seemed not to notice. Her interest in the opposite sex was almost nonexistent and seemingly nonessential. Although she had a couple of close girl friends, most of the boys saw her as this nerdy little girl who would rather study than socialize, so for the most part they left her alone. She shunned makeup and fancy hairdos and up-to- date clothing. Most days her hair was bound in a simple ponytail held with a simple colored band. Maybe not having a mother had something to do with that, but Jennifer preferred to be as inconspicuous as possible. The only exception--she wore the same small pearl earrings almost everyday. They were a gift from her father, made from one of her mother's necklaces.

Jennifer may have played the part of the nerd in school, but she didn't look it. She had bright vivid blue eyes that seemed to be earnestly interested in the world around her. She was pretty in a plain way. Her hair color was somewhere between brown and blonde and she had wonderful dimples that just seemed to magically form in the hollows of her cheeks when she smiled. She was petite and thin, but her hips had the roundness that comes with womanhood and her breasts although small seemed to be in direct proportion to her small frame. She dressed conservatively preferring blouses and skirts, but in the summer months she was often seen in shorts and tee shirts, usually riding her old Schwinn bicycle wherever she went.

Her high school years finally behind her, Jennifer graduated at the top of her class and went on to St. Theresa's College a half a state away,

The Magic Book

on a full academic scholarship, and pursued her dream to become a librarian.

College, however, was a whole new ball game for Jennifer. For all of her growing up years she had been driven each day to school, and picked up each afternoon by her loving father, but now she was two hundred miles away. It took two tries, but she took the test and finally got her drivers license. Her father bought her a three-year-old dark green Honda, but except for coming back home on the weekends it sat in her dormitory parking lot.

There was another big change in college for Jenny and that came from her peers. In high school she had been the smartest of the smartest, but here in college, she was just one of a large group of honor students. That status--- that lonely girl at the top who once was almost an attraction, had changed, and she was now just one of the group. No one seemed to notice or care if you were smart or average in college. No more 'atta girls' from the teachers. No more prideful smiles from her doting father. So for that reason Jennifer seemed to take it easier academically, and although still an achiever, now she read more for recreation than for learning.

She was still the virgin she had always been; chaste and pure, and hanging onto that virtue like a badge of honor. Boys were little threat as they didn't seem to notice her much anyway, and if they did, her actions quickly discouraged them. She was saving herself for someone special and had no interest in tarnishing herself, or her reputation. Oh she had sensuous thoughts from time to time as all girls do. Many of the books she read would have love scenes in them, some of them graphically describing the act of human mating. But even though the thoughts and words of the books caused her face to flush, her juices to flow, and her heart to race, she never allowed herself to act on these thoughts either with someone, or by herself. It just would ruin everything, she reasoned.

At the start of her senior year her father took ill, and at first even though she worried about him, he insisted that he would be fine in time. That things had just gotten out of sync in his aging body and he just needed a little period of adjustment. She drove home from school almost every weekend to see him. After all, he was all she had. Her aunt Rita, her dad's sister, who lived in the same city, told Jennifer she would care for her brother and keep her informed about his health. With each visit home for her, however, he seemed to look more gaunt and grew more lethargic. He would smile and seem to draw strength from somewhere each time Jenny came to visit. But it soon became evident that her dad was not going to get better, and Aunt Rita, herself a widow, came to stay taking over Jenny's old bedroom with all of its books.

It was just before Christmas vacation that Aunt Rita called one snowy evening and told Jennifer she should hurry home. Her father wanted her to be with him and for the first time he was acknowledging his demise. She drove back home in a raging snowstorm, crying so hard she had to stop from time to time, just to compose herself. She was sad but more than that she was also scared. He had been the bulwark in her life, her pillar of strength, which had kept her from the evils of the world. If he died she would be all alone, an orphan thrown to the mercies of what ever came her way. She had no other men in her life and for that matter outside of Aunt Rita, no women either. She felt almost naked and exposed.

Jenny was bereft and overwhelmed with grief. Her father was the one person she had felt would always be there for her, and now facing up to what lay ahead, she didn't have a clue about what she was going to do.

Aunt Rita met her at the door and took her in her arms. For a few seconds she soaked up the compassion, but then looking over Rita's shoulder she saw the hospital bed in the living room and the nurse sitting by his bedside reading. She walked over to his bed tentatively. Maybe she was afraid of what she was going to see and maybe it was just that she had never seen anyone dying before and had no idea of the process.

The nurse stood up and said, "I'll leave you alone for a while. He seems to be comfortable right now but I doubt he will see the night out." Jenny didn't acknowledge that she had heard her but sat down on the chair and took his hand. He appeared to be sleeping but the moment she said "Dad," he opened his eyes and smiled. His hand squeezed hers and those bright blue eyes that had always been his trademark sparkled.

"Jenny," he said. "Thank heavens. I was so afraid I wouldn't be able to say goodbye."

"Dad," she blurted out and collapsed onto the bedclothes sobbing. "Oh my God, Daddy what am I going to do without you?"

With what little strength he had left he reached down and took her tear stained face in his hands. "Jenny I have loved you like no father could ever love his daughter. Now it is up to you to share that love with someone special. Promise me you will do that."

Still she skirted the subject. "Daddy please know, that you were the best father a girl could have. I love you with all of my heart."

He smiled and closed his eyes. Then he took a deep breath, exhaled, and his chest did not rise again. Jenny could only watch for him to breath once more, but she knew he was gone. For a long time she just held his hand while Aunt Rita came and cried softly with her, her own arms wrapped around Jenny from behind. There were no words, it had all been said.

The next day, and the few days after, there was a blur of friends and family, hot dishes and hugs, and reminiscing. Jenny was grief stricken, but from somewhere she found the strength to talk with all of them, and then suddenly it was just her and Aunt Rita walking away from the grave site where she had buried her father the day before, and came back one last time to say goodbye. She dropped Rita off at her house and gave her a big hug. She had stayed with Rita during the wake and the funeral, and the steady flow of friends and family had kept her mind occupied. It gave her less time for self-pity, but now there was the problem of the house and her dad's possessions. She had only one more day to spare, and then she had to be back at college for mid-term exams.

"I'll come back in a couple of weeks and we can talk about the house and Dad's things. I'm going over there now to spend the night, and then I have to get back to school. Thank you so much," she sobbed, and buried her face in her aunt's shoulder.

"Go in peace child," she said. "He's with your mother now. All of those years and he never was unfaithful to her." They kissed and Jennifer got back in the car and drove off.

It was only about ten miles to her childhood home from Aunt Rita's house, but the traffic was bad that morning and that provided some time to sit and think. She needed to secure the house and find one of the neighbors to keep an eye on it until she could get back. Jennifer's thoughts were all over the place but mostly about the house, and her father, and a wave of grief came over her and she started crying again. She noticed people in the next car watching her so she tried her best to compose herself, there would be a time for serious crying later, but it wasn't now. It was so unfair when you didn't have time to grieve.

It was noon when she nosed her Honda up the single lane drive and parked along side of the white clapboard house, with its faded red shutters. All of the drapes and shades were drawn and it looked so deserted. She walked back down the driveway to the mailbox, which was overflowing with papers and envelopes. It had a red sticker on it from the post office stating that if the box was not cleaned out that delivery would be stopped. There were two gray garbage containers sitting at the end of the driveway, one of them lying on its side. Jennifer sorted through the mail and deposited the bulk of it in one of them and then pulled them both up by the garage. She made a mental note to call the post office and the garbage company and stop the services.

For a brief moment she stood and looked out over the small backyard. The rusty old swing set and the over grown sand box, that hadn't been used for fifteen years or better, were still there. Her father hadn't been good at getting rid of things. An old birdhouse with its roof gone sat at a slight angle on a grey weathered four-by-four wooden pole. A peek through the window in the service door and into the garage showed her fathers old gray Buick parked inside. She would have to try and sell it. She tried the door and it was open so she turned the button to make it lock, but didn't go inside.

For the first time she noticed the cold on her face and a few snow flurries coming down. She walked back to the steps of the house making another mental note to have someone keep the driveway shoveled when it snowed.

The back door stuck a little and Jenny used her foot to push it open once she had unlocked it. There was a rag rug inside the door and she sat at the kitchen table took off her shoes and left them there on the rug. The floors were cold, the house smelled musty and damp, and it was as gloomy inside, as her life felt right now. She went into the front room and pulled the drapes back and the cold daylight spilled in. She sat down in her dad's favorite chair and tenderly fingered his pipe. A television guide lay on the coffee table, along with a book. Jenny picked the book up and turned it over. It was a book her dad had bought for her when she was in high school, 'Catcher in the Rye.' For a brief moment she tried to remember what it was about and then remembered it was about a boy in college much like she was right now.

She looked around the room at the pictures she remembered so well. The spot in the carpet where she had spilled kool-aid that never came out, and the afghan she had made four Christmas's ago was still neatly folded on the top of the couch. It was cold in the house and she went over and turned up the thermostat and heard the furnace click on. Taking the afghan down and covering herself, she curled up on the couch. Finally it was crying time.

It was the middle of the night when she awoke, after crying herself asleep. Jenny went out into the kitchen to try and find something to drink. Her throat was sore from sobbing, and her eyes were red and swollen. At least it was warm in the house now. She found some hot chocolate mix and heated some water on the stove. When she opened the refrigerator it was dark and she saw the plug lying out of the receptacle on the counter. Aunt Rita had cleaned it out for her.

The urge to relieve herself now came over her and Jenny went down the short hall to the bathroom. When she flicked on the switch the fluorescent light came on with that same humming noise it always made. The toilet bowel was nearly dry, so she flushed it once to get water back in it and sat down to do her business. Reaching in front of her she pulled the shower curtain back. A bottle of shampoo still sat on the edge of the tub and a bath mat was curled up in the bottom.

Jenny went back to the kitchen where her water was boiling and made her drink. She dug through the cupboards for something to eat, and finally settled for a box of Ritz crackers, as the cupboards were nearly empty. She was trying to work up the courage to go to her bedroom. The room that had been her safe haven for so many years growing up. With her crackers and cup in a saucer she walked down the hallway. Both her door and her fathers' door were closed. She opened her fathers first. The bed was made and the room was clean and the oval picture of her parents still sat on the nightstand. She picked it up and kissed it softly and then put it back. Jenny went back to her door and opened it and reaching in turned on the light. The little lamp beside her bed with the white frilly lampshade came on. It bathed the room in soft light accenting all of the bookshelves and books she had collected over the years.

Jenny sat on the end of the bed, lethargic and emotionally exhausted. For a few minutes she sat and reacquainted herself with all of her dolls and books, and things she had collected over the years. Looking at her watch she saw it was one-thirty in the morning. *I should go to bed and get up early I, have a big day tomorrow,* she thought. She found some old pajamas and undressed and slid under the covers. Then she reached over and shut off the lamp and wave after wave of sobs filled her chest once more, until she could cry no more and she finally fell asleep.

The next morning she paid the utility bills that had been in the mail. Then she called Mr. Parcells, who was retired and had lived next door for twenty years, and after going on how sorry he was for her dad's death, he said he would take care of the place until she came back in a couple of weeks. She felt better this morning more relaxed and more in control. By noon she was done with her mourning so she turned the heat down, pulled the drapes closed once more, and closed and locked the door behind her. She would stop at the post office and get the mail forwarded to her, but first she walked over to Mr. Parcells and left the key.

Back on the road she was going home to the only home she had right now; St. Theresa's College, almost two hundred miles away.

CHAPTER TWO

Jenny started working in the college library as an intern right after Christmas. It was work she liked and had always dreamed about, but the people she was working for left a lot to be desired. Oh well, she thought it would be something to put on her resume someday, and heaven knows she needed that. She had only a few months of school left and then she would be out job hunting. She was still on the dean's list academically, but it didn't seem that important to her any more. She knew she couldn't be the head of the list, so why try that hard, and with her dad gone, there was no one to cheer her on.

This weekend she was going back home to pack up the rest of her stuff and meet with the auction people about getting rid of her father's estate. The house had been transferred into her name, so she was free to sell it whenever she wanted to. Her father had seen to it that his simple will was all in order, so things were happening fast. For a brief time she even thought about going back there to live, but the neighborhood had gone downhill, and she really didn't want to live there anyway. There were too many memories, and too few jobs in that area.

Jenny rented a small truck from a U-haul company and bought some shipping boxes and set out for the house on a crisp cold day in February. By Sunday morning the truck was full and she headed for a storage unit she had rented not far from the college. The house was being sold and the auction was next weekend. There would be little reason to return after that.

Life for Jenny was very simple and routine: Go to school, go to work, and go home to her cramped dormitory room. She had no close friends and very few she could even call acquaintances, but that seemed to be the way she wanted it.

In June she received her diploma and an offer to stay on at the library until she found work. It was the summer of 1974 and the country was in the troughs of a major recession. Jobs were scarce for everyone, and especially for librarians. There were many of them applying for every job opening that was advertised and most with more experience. She thought she could stay at the college longer but the head librarian didn't like Jenny, so on one cool October day, she gave her two months to find work, and then her job with the college would be over.

Every evening she sat with the paper and a highlighter and followed the want ads. In six weeks, she was able to find only six librarian jobs, and experienced people filled all of them as fast as she found out about them. She had the degree and the desire; she just didn't know how to sell herself when the opportunity did present itself. Dejected, she didn't know what she was going to do when her job was over. To add insult to injury, when that time came she would also lose her privilege of living on campus.

There was some money in Jenny's bank account that could hold her over for a while. But her real hope was that the money that had come from the sale of her father's house would someday buy her a home in a quiet neighborhood, where she could live in peace and quiet with all of her books, and maybe Mr. Right, if there was one out there. Yes Jenny was starting to think about men…but like a job-- where to find one? She was tired of being lonely, but she wasn't going to relax her standards. She wasn't that lonely. She didn't go to bars and she didn't belong to a church. She was so shy and withdrawn most men thought something was wrong with her.

On a Sunday afternoon in early November, only days before her job ended, something caught Jenny's eye. It was a small ad in the St. Paul paper for a bookstore for sale in St. Paul. She went to the front desk in the library and got a pencil and paper and wrote down the phone number. The price was within her budget, and it was advertised with living quarters above it. Never In her wildest dreams had she thought beyond being a librarian, but here was a chance to be surrounded by books. What more could she ask for?

The Magic Book

Jenny couldn't wait to get back to her room to call the realtor. What had seemed foolish for a while was starting to seem to be a better idea by the minute. She thought only about the pluses: being her own boss and not having to listen to orders from others and filling her bank account instead of someone else's. Her hands were trembling as she sat at the little desk in her dorm room and dialed the number for Advance Reality. The realtors name was Jerry Dressel.

"Yes," he said, "the store was still for sale and had been for quite some time."

"When can I see it?" she asked.

"Well Wednesday would be a good day," Jerry replied.

"Wednesday. That's three days off. You're not going to sell it to someone else before then are you?"

He laughed a haughty laugh. "I hardly think so dear."

Jenny made an appointment to be at his office Wednesday at one. *He had sounded almost condescending,* she thought. *Was he serious or not?*

It was better than a three-hour drive from the college to St. Paul, so Jenny was up at the crack of dawn to make the trip. It sure would be nice if it worked out and she was living back in the Twin Cities, but she had learned not get too excited about things until they actually happened.

The countryside of south central Minnesota passed by her car window for mile after mile. She saw many farms with multiple big blue Harvester silos and empty fields now waiting for next springs planting. There were very few standing crops left, so most of the fields were endless furrows of turned over black dirt and corn stubble from this years crop. There were very few trees around, except for around the farm buildings that appeared as little oasis's in this vast prairie land.

It was freeway most of the way so she had to exit at one small hamlet to get coffee and use the restroom at a gas station convenience store. She gave the woman a dollar bill and told her to keep the change for the fifty-cent coffee. The woman, who was watching two little kids that were playing on the floor behind her, looked haggard and tired. *That was not ever going to be her,* thought Jenny.

From time to time she would think about all the times she had driven home to see her dad, and a couple of times she caught herself on the verge of crying. Oh how she wished he was here to help her with this. He would know all of the right things to do. But if he were here, she wouldn't have the money to do it anyway.

Finally the familiar buildings and stores of the South St. Paul suburbs came into view and Jenny glanced down at her watch. It was just noon so she had plenty of time. A half hour later she drove into the parking lot of the reality building and shut off the Honda. She had made a peanut butter and jelly sandwich, and had brought a can of soda along, so she sat in her car in the parking lot and ate her lunch. When she was done eating she looked in the rearview mirror, fixed her makeup, adjusted the pearl studs in her ears, and walked into the building.

"Can I help you?" a heavyset matronly looking woman, with her eye glasses hanging on gold chains that only seemed to point attention to her ample bosom, asked from a desk that said Receptionist.

"I have an appointment to see Jerry Dressel," Jenny said.

The lady stood and walked down a short hall to another office and said something through the doorway that Jenny didn't understand.

"He'll be right out," she said, smiling as she returned.

Jenny had pictured Jerry Dressel as old and paunchy so she was surprised when a middle age man, that was quite handsome, came out and took her hand. "So you want to look at the old Albertson Book Store?" he asked.

She smiled and nodded her head.

"Hi I'm Jerry," he said

"Jennifer Crawford," she answered.

"Well, let's take my car and run over there, it's just a couple of miles." He was putting on his hat and coat as he talked. "Come from far?" he asked.

St. Theresa's College," Jenny answered.

He looked at her quizzically. "That's in southwestern Minnesota isn't it Jennifer, or can I call you Jenny?"

"Yes, please do. It's by the South Dakota border," she said.

"Wow you did have quite a trip. I hope it's worth it for you?"

"I hope so too," she said.

On the way over to the store Jerry gave her some pictures to look at and told her about the store. His car was a new Cadillac and Jenny had never ridden in anything this fancy. She didn't comment on it, but she was impressed.

"The store has been closed for two years," Jerry explained, "so it's going to be dirty and dusty. The previous owner, who by the way had been the only owner, died of old age, and his family is anxious to sell it. With the economy the way it is, there haven't been many lookers. You might get a bargain if the financing works out for you."

Jenny didn't tell him she had the money, all she said was, "I hope so."

The store was right downtown in St. Paul, sandwiched between two multi- story office buildings that were also turn-of-the-century. Jerry pointed the store out as they passed by, and then he drove down about a block and parked in a ramp. It was dark and noisy in the ramp, with lots of cars coming and going, but soon they stepped out of the elevator and exited out onto the sidewalk.

For a moment they stood in front of the old building and Jenny looked at the almost century old structure. The front window had once said 'Albertson's Books,' but one of the o's and the k had fallen down and now it just said Albertson's Bo s. The windows were papered over halfway up so you couldn't see inside and the paper was yellowed, water stained, and falling down in places.

Jerry unlocked and opened the wooden door and some simple bells on the door tinkled as they stepped inside. "Hang on and I'll get the lights," he said. He had gone to the far wall behind a counter where an ancient cash register, with the word <u>National</u> on it in big silver letters, was perched on top of it. He threw some switches and three rows of fluorescent lights flickered and came on. About half of the bulbs were burned out but she could see down the narrow aisles all the way to the back of the store. Outside, the sound of sirens became louder and louder and then faded away.

Jenny walked up and down the aisles looking at all of the books. The shelves were about half full. The shelves themselves were sturdy, had been stained, and appeared to be oak. They looked to be in good shape. Each unit was about five shelves high and if she stood on her tiptoes she could just reach the top. At the end of the aisle was a sitting area with two old couches and some over-stuffed chairs. A handwritten sign on the wall said, "Please return books to where you found them on the shelves." Another one said, "This not a library, but feel free to browse." Behind the furniture there was a half wall and set of steps that went up to the second level. She looked up the stairs at a small landing and a wooden door that had a Private sign on it.

Jerry, who had been following her quietly, said, "That's the living quarters up there, do you want to see them?"

Jenny nodded her head. "In a moment," she said.

She walked up and down all five aisles stopping to examine a few of the books. Some of then appeared to be recent copies, but there were some old ones that appeared to be worn and used. "He must have sold old and used books," she said out loud.

"Looks that way," Jerry said. "Do you know a lot about books?"

"Yes I have a degree in English Literature and I studied to be a librarian."

"Why the interest in the book store?" he asked.

Jenny didn't want to tell him the real reason, so she said. "I don't know, it just seemed interesting."

The flooring in the building was wooden and very dirty. The ceiling appeared to be some kind of metal panels about a foot square that were embossed. They had been painted, and the paint was peeling off some of them, and a few of them seemed to be coming loose, giving the appearance of a three quarter tear. The store smelled musty, but at the same time not really damp. Just old and musty even though it was quite warm in there.

"Is there a basement?" Jenny asked.

"Yes, but it's small and meant only for the boiler and the hot water heater. It's under the stairs in the back. They did tell me the heating appliances were fairly new."

She had forgotten about the heating plant, but now she saw the radiators that were cut into the shelving in the two side aisles. She walked over and put her hand on one of them and it was warm, and she could feel water pulsing through it. A hissing sound came from the valve on the end of it and there was some build up of mineral deposit around it. There was a lot she didn't know about taking care of a building. She had never had to do any of that before. Her dad was always there.

Suddenly she remembered the upstairs. *Living quarters were almost as important as the business right now,* she thought. "Can I see the upstairs now?" she asked.

Jerry had been following her around but remained fairly quiet. It was almost as if he wasn't that interested in selling it, or maybe he had an idea that she wasn't all that interested or probably couldn't afford it anyway, so why waste the energy, but Jenny asking to go upstairs seemed to wake him up.

"Yes. Sure," he said. "Lets go upstairs."

Jerry led the way up the creaky steps. Jenny could smell his cologne and see his broad back. She had forgotten she was alone in an old building in St. Paul with a man she didn't even know, but she was seemingly at ease with him, despite the fact they were going to some out of the way place in the building.

The door opened into a small kitchen with a row of white metal appliances that dated back to World War II. There was a small table and two chairs beside one wall but otherwise the room was empty. In the middle of the upstairs was a large gathering area that was carpeted in green shag. There were indents in the rug where furniture must have sat for a long time. The room was big; it looked to be about fifty feet long. There was no furniture visible, and a lot of the room was taken up with boxes and boxes of books. On the far end of the room was a door, and it led to a bedroom that looked out over the busy street below. This room too was empty and the shades were up. Jenny walked over and looked down at the cars and buses going by below. To the left was an open door and Jenny could see into a small bathroom. She walked over and stood in the doorway. It had a sink on the wall with a medicine cabinet above it with a cracked mirror. A commode that was almost black with water stains was at one end, and a big bathtub with claw legs sat on the other end. The floor was white tile and a couple of those were cracked or missing. There was a small window that faced the street but the shade was drawn and you would have to stand in the tub to see out of it. Jerry had stayed out in the gathering area, so Jenny walked back out to him.

"A lot to absorb." he said.

"Yes it is. Can I have a few days to think it over?"

"Certainly. It's not going anywhere," he said, almost sarcastically.

They walked back through the store and Jenny stopped to look around once more. Jerry asked her if she was done and she answered, "For now."

He seemed to be in a hurry. He shut off the lights and locked the door and they walked back to the ramp in silence except for Jerry to say. "It wouldn't hurt to make an offer. I'm not sure how low they will go, but I know they want to get rid of it."

Nice choice of words, Jenny thought.

When they got back to the office he handed her his business card while they were still in the car. "Call me if there is anything else you want to know, or if you want to make an offer."

"I know the former owner is dead," Jenny said, "but do you think I could talk to someone who had anything to do with the store?"

"Give me your number and if there is someone, I'll find out and have them call you. If I remember right, there was daughter who worked with him. Anything else?"

"Not right now."

He held out his hand. "Thanks Jenny. I'll be in touch."

She drove away with a strange feeling about the whole day. She had expected some high-pressure salesman, not someone that didn't seem to care one-way or the other. She nosed the Honda out of the parking lot, heading for the freeway and home.

CHAPTER THREE

The drive home went by fast. Her mind was trying to process everything she had seen and heard and she was deep in thought. *The building was old and run down but a quick look told her many of the books were worth a lot of money. To live right in the middle of downtown didn't seem to be very attractive, but maybe she would get used to it. Dad would have never allowed her to act like this, but maybe that was the difference now. Dad wasn't here and his little girl was in charge now, wasn't she?*

It would take a lot of work, and a fair amount of money to make the place look attractive, and did anyone go to these types of bookstores anymore? If she could get them to come down in price a little maybe she would have some money left over for fixing the place up. Could she do some of it, and hire some of it done? Why not, and where was she getting all of this courage all of a sudden? Her dad had, in some ways, never let his little girl grow up and now---well it felt good. It felt like she was truly becoming independent. Tonight she would call Aunt Rita and tell her the news.

She had driven less than a hundred miles when she finally made up her mind. *What did she have to lose? The property it sat on had to be worth more than they were asking for the store,* she thought. *Many of those books she had seen were rare. Some of them even first editions, yes, she would make them an offer. First though she wanted to talk to someone from the family.*

Jenny returned to the college and her dorm room around suppertime, and her stomach told her she had had too little to eat that day. She opened a can of soup, poured it into a bowl with some water and put it in the microwave. She marveled at how this newfound appliance heated her food, but it would be really nice to have a kitchen with a stove where she could cook and bake. Something the school didn't allow.

She had just poured her soup into a large coffee mug and grabbed a slice of bread when the phone rang. Jenny didn't get many calls but she wiped her hands on her pants and picked up the receiver. A feminine sounding voice asked if she was speaking to Jennifer Crawford.

"Yes," Jenny answered, "who is this?"

"My name is Caroline Finch and I'm the daughter of John Albertson, the man who owned the bookstore you looked at today. The realtor asked me to call you. He said you had some questions."

"Yes. Yes I did," she stammered. "You caught me a little of guard here and now I don't remember everything I wanted to ask you, but one of the things was, did you work for your father?"

"I did for many years, at least until I got married and started having kids. What was it you wanted to know pertaining to that?"

"Well let me tell you my situation. I have just graduated from college and I was going to try and be a librarian, but there are no jobs right now, so I thought with my love for books, maybe this would be a good second choice for a career." Almost out of breath she paused for a second. "My problem is I have never worked in the public sector and have no experience at all with this kind of a venture. Could you, or would you, help me get started, if I bought the store?"

"You are able to afford to buy the store?" Caroline's tone sounded skeptical.

"Yes. My father just passed away and left me some money."

"I'm sorry about your father," she said, "but getting back to your request, I think we could work something out. My kids are grown now so I do have the time. It might be fun to go back there for a while."

"That would help me a lot. Oh thank you. Was your dad's business profitable?" Jenny asked.

"Yes, I would say so, but he dealt a lot in old books and collectors items. He was an expert in those things. I'm not so sure you would have the expertise to do that, but there are a lot of things that could be done with that store. I think if you're serious, then make an offer for the store and then we could meet someplace and talk in length about this whole issue."

"That sounds good," Jenny said. "I would like that. Any idea how much you have to have? I know that sounds stupid, but I need to know what to offer you to make this work. As I said I have some money but not a lot of it."

Caroline laughed. "I think the family would accept something in the range of ten percent less than we were asking, but you work that out with the realtor and then we can talk some more."

"Thanks," Jenny said. "I'll be in touch."

Now she was really excited. She grabbed a pencil and paper and started crunching some numbers. They were asking two hundred and fifty thousand. Ten percent from that-- well that was easy. She looked in her checkbook. With savings, checking, and certificates she had three hundred and fifteen thousand. If she gave them two twenty-five she would have ninety left to fix the place up and live on until she could open the store.

Jenny sat at the table bouncing her pencil on its eraser and catching it. It was a big step, but then again, she might never get an opportunity like this again. On the other hand she could go broke and then she would have an old decaying empty bookstore. She took out her wallet and retrieved the business card Jerry had given her this morning.

To heck with it. She was tired of being so conservative, and she was going for it.

The next morning Jenny waited until almost noon to call Jerry at the reality office. She didn't want to seem to be too anxious, and she wanted to think about it for a while longer. It was a big step. But all of the reasoning in the world could not dampen her enthusiasm, so she made the call.

That same sweet lady she had seen yesterday at the reception desk answered the phone.

"Hi, is Jerry in?" Jenny asked.

"He is. Who shall I tell him is calling?"

"Tell him its Jennifer Crawford."

Jerry answered the phone before she had time to think about what she was going to say. "Jennifer, how are you?"

"I'm fine. Mr. Dressel I've made up my mind to make an offer on the store."

"Ah, yes the book store--- let me get that sheet here. Here it is. Are you familiar with how we do this?"

"No I'm afraid not."

"Well I'll have Charlotte get the papers out to you right away today and you should have them tomorrow, Wednesday at the latest. You fill in the highlighted areas with your figures and send them back to me. I'll present your offer to the owners and by next week I should have an answer for you. Did you speak with the daughter?"

"I did and she was very helpful."

"Well I guess that's all there is to it then. Any questions?"

"Not right now. But if I do have some, I can call you right?"

"Absolutely. Don't hesitate, and thanks Jennifer. –Oh before I forget, do you know who you will be using for financing if they accept your offer?"

"There won't be any financing necessary."

Jerry let out a low whistle and then wished he hadn't. This could go fast he thought to himself.

Jenny looked up at the calendar. She worked tonight and then she had five days left. Today was the fifteenth and she had to be out of her dorm on the last day of the month. She hadn't slept much last night and with all that had happened, she was exhausted. She needed a nap. Tomorrow would be soon enough to call Aunt Rita.

The papers came Wednesday and they were self-explanatory. She filled them out and got them back in the mail. On Friday morning Caroline Finch called Jenny to tell her they would accept her offer. Then Jerry called that afternoon to ask her when she could come in to work out the details. *It was all going so fast. Aunt Rita was in Mexico on vacation so that conversation was out, but there was nothing Rita could have done to talk her out of it at this late stage anyway.*

They set up the meeting for the following Friday at Jerry's office. Jenny cashed in her certificates and purchased a cashier check for two hundred and twenty five thousand dollars.

She told the library she wouldn't be able to work any more and today would be her last day. They didn't' seem to care, and for the first time Jenny didn't care either. She arranged for her belongings, stored at the storage locker, to be loaded into a truck next week Thursday. On the day after she was moving out, and back to the cities, and until she got in the store she would live with Rita. Her twenty year old cousin Chad, Rita's son, was going to go back with her to help her move and drive the truck. Chad and she had not been close growing up, but he was the only person she knew that would help her. She didn't know of any other men she could ask for help. *Heck she didn't know any other men, period.*

The only people at the meeting that morning were Jerry the realtor, Caroline Finch and her husband, and a man from the title company. The meeting was over in twenty minutes and Jenny now owned a bookstore in downtown St. Paul. She received three sets of keys, a portfolio full of papers, and a promise from Caroline that she would meet with her as soon as she was settled.

Jenny drove slowly out of the parking lot and headed for downtown. Her mind was buzzing with all that had gone on and all that there was still left to do. There were so many details left, it was almost overwhelming, but she did her best to calm herself down and think rationally. *She had to get the utilities in her name, and arrange for insurance. She needed to get the phone hooked back up. She would need to find a contractor to help with some of the remodeling. She needed to talk with book suppliers, and maybe Christine could shed some light on that, if she still would work with her, now that she had her money.*

Jenny had no plans to open the store for at least a month. In fact it might even take longer then that to put things in order. Maybe she wouldn't find help right away. It wasn't like people were just sitting around waiting for her to call.

Just for this afternoon she was going to walk around the store and make a list and put together a plan, and than she would pick up Chad at Aunt Rita's and head back to the school.

As she parked her car in the same ramp her and Jerry had been in the other day she had a strange concern. Where would she keep her car? The ramp was not a solution. She got out her notebook and wrote: Find a parking space.

Jenny stood on the sidewalk with the store keys in her hand, studying the buildings' exterior. The paint was chipping and there was a crack in one of the front windows. The bricks had places where the mortar was missing and there were bolts sticking out of the wall where a sign must have hung. She didn't recall seeing any of this the other day. Sometimes enthusiasm, like love can put blinders on you.

Once inside the store she remembered where the switches were and turned the lights on and noticed immediately that the switches were housed in metal boxes instead of recessed into the wall. Was electricity an add-on in this building? Ugly metal conduit snaked its way up to the rows of lights above. The light directly over her head flickered, came on and then went off. The musty smell she had noticed the other day seemed more intense. Would she ever be able to make the place smell fresh again? She pushed the keys on the cash register but they all seemed to be jammed.

Walking to the back of the store she saw the door under the stairs that went to the basement. Opening the door she found the switch, and a single light bulb suspended from a dangling wire came on, illuminating a small room maybe fifteen by twelve. She walked tentatively down the steps hanging onto a crude wooden railing and stopped at the bottom step swiping at a spider web in front of her face. A somewhat modern furnace in front of her ran quietly and she could see the blue gas flame of the burner through a hole that seemed to be there for that purpose. To her right was a white water heater that looked to be almost new, but there was a wet spot on the floor where something had been dripping. Something clicked and the furnace flame went out. Looking around without walking farther into the room the rest of it appeared to be empty. Uncomfortable in the basement, she went back upstairs and closed the door. She wrote another note in her book: Have the heating plant serviced.

The more she walked around, the more over-whelming the task of getting the place in shape again seemed to be. She had been upstairs, and now coming back down into the store again, she saw a door she hadn't noticed before. It was almost hidden in the corner behind some boxes of books. Jenny tried the knob and the heavy steel door creaked opened. She was looking into the alley at a dumpster, and space with enough room to park a couple of cars. She went back to the list that was now about twenty items long and crossed off the first one. She had her parking space and hey-- something off her list.

Jenny looked at her watch. She had told Aunt Rita and Chad that she would be there for supper and it was almost five. Taking one last look around, she gave out a loud sigh. It was going to be a lot of work and she hoped she was up to it. Her enthusiasm had been dampened just a bit.

Aunt Rita had cooked a pot roast with lots of varieties of vegetables, and Jenny who was starved ate her fill. It had been a long time since she had a home cooked meal like this. The conversation was light and Rita seemed to be supportive of her new adventure. She had once worked in a bookstore herself, and she thought it was an interesting way to make living. She was just glad to see her niece doing so well, so soon after losing her father, but then she hadn't seen Jenny's store yet.

Chad picked at his food and said little. Jenny could sense that the idea for him to help her had not been his idea. He was dressed in some old army clothes and wore his long hair down around his shoulders. It was greasy and unkempt. *No wonder he couldn't get a job*, she thought.

The ride back to the college was quiet. Chad was polite, but quiet, and slept most of the way. It was dark when they got there so they went right to the dorm and Jenny made coffee. They talked a little about their childhood, but they had so few things in common the conversation soon reached a lull. She gave Chad some blankets and a pillow and showed him how to make the couch up. He was busy watching her tiny television and ignored her for the most part. She took a shower and went to bed. It had been a long day.

Jenny had the majority of her belongings packed and it didn't take long for her to pack the rest. It was nine-thirty in the morning already and she was anxious to get going. Chad was still sleeping on the couch, on top of the blankets she had brought out, one hand shoved down the front of his pants. When she woke him, he seemed to be irritated but didn't say much. He went to the bathroom and urinated loudly with the door half open. He said he didn't want anything to eat or drink.

The truck was right where the man said it would be. The storage locker was empty and open. All of Jenny's belongings from the dorm were packed in her Honda. "You follow me," she said to Chad. "When we get to St. Paul we'll have to park in the alley behind the store, and I haven't been back there yet, so be patient while I find the way. Do you need anything?"

"I might stop at the first convenience store we see to get something to munch on. I'm a little short of cash do you have any you could give me?"

Jenny took a five-dollar-bill from her purse and gave it to him. He started the truck and put it into gear. "Let's go," he said. He seemed impatient.

It seemed sad to leave the little campus and the town she had grown to see as home for the last four years, but there was nothing here for her anymore.

They stopped at a convenience store that also sold liquor just outside of town and Chad came out with a brown paper bag. Jenny could only guess what was in it. She just hoped he made it to St. Paul in one piece with her furniture and possessions. She was glad they were in separate vehicles.

She was weary of the same drive to St. Paul for the fourth time in two weeks, and for the first time she seemed to not notice the surrounding landscape. Jenny had started out in the lead, but Chad quickly passed her and she had to go almost seventy-five miles an hour to keep up. About half way there he pulled over on the shoulder and got out of the truck and urinated next to it, oblivious of the cars going by. She could only watch, astonished that anyone would behave this way.

When they approached the city, Chad fell back and let her take the lead again. Soon they were coming down Interstate 94 and she could see the dome of the Capital off to the left. They exited on Maryland and when she came to St. Peter Street she drove by the store and made a cautious left turn. There was the alley. It was narrow but clean and uncluttered. Two stores down there was a small parking lot, so she stopped and told Chad, who was behind her, to back up to the steel door behind the bookstore. For the time being she parked next door. One of the keys on the ring opened the rusty door and it opened with a loud screech.

The only furniture Jenny had was her bed, one dresser, and a small dressing table. It was packed in the back of the truck and she and Chad managed to get it up the steps into the kitchen area. His breath was rank and smelled of alcohol and cigarettes as he walked behind her down the stairs. He made no attempt to walk though the store and said or asked nothing.

The Magic Book

They left her boxes of books downstairs in the back along with the rest of the things from the truck, and most of the things that were in her car. Soon the truck was empty, as well as the car, so Jenny said to Chad. "The place where we leave the truck is over by the Capital next to Sears. I'll follow you and then take you home."

On the way back out to Aunt Rita's she gave Chad fifty dollars. "Is that enough?" she asked.

He stuffed the money in his jacket pocket and said, "Thanks."

The house was dark when they got to her aunts, so she left Chad off in the driveway. "Thanks again," she said. "I don't know what I would have done without you."

He smiled, and said, "Have a good life."

It was suppertime when she got back to the store. She parked her car and went inside, but felt that if she didn't eat soon her knees were going to buckle. Jenny walked through the store and out the front door to a small café next door.

She ordered a cheeseburger in a basket, something she rarely ate, but right now she needed some comfort food. The café was warm, and nice, and the crowd seemed subdued. *Maybe someday some of these people would be her customers too,* she thought.

Back home at the store Jenny put her bed together and wrestled the box spring and the mattress on top of it. She had a few basic tools she had taken from her dad's garage before the estate sale. She found the box with bedding and brought it upstairs and put some towels in the bathroom. She was going to have to go shopping in the morning for food and cleaning supplies. As it stood she didn't even have toilet paper and right now she was tired beyond her comprehension. At least the bed was familiar and the blankets smelled familiar and good. For a while she thought about all of the things she had to do and it seemed overwhelming. Then she decided to think about something else she had neglected, and she thought about her dad for the first time in days. "Daddy please help me," Jenny said out-loud and then went to bed and cried herself to sleep.

CHAPTER FOUR

Sometime during the night a noisy truck with its back up horn blaring, awakened her, and Jenny got up and went to the window. It was a city truck hauling away snow off the city streets. It looked to be very cold outside and she could see the men's foggy breath as they stood by the truck talking. A drink of water suddenly sounded good and she padded out to the kitchen and ran the faucet a while to clean out the pipe, and then with no glass handy, drank right out of the faucet. She had no idea where a glass was right now. The running water brought something else to mind and she headed to the bathroom. It disgusted her to have to sit on that brown stained stool and tomorrow morning as soon as she got some cleaning supplies it was getting clean.

Jenny slept fitfully the rest of the night. It was going to take some getting used to as far as the noise was concerned. Directly across the street was a rundown hotel, and its neon sign flashing on and off caused a reddish hue to fall over her bedroom each time it lit. She made a mental note to get some room darkening shades while she was shopping.

The next morning bright and early Jenny went to Sears and filled a cart full of cleaning, things, paper products, and painting supplies. Her plan right now was to get her living quarters habitable, and worry about the store later. While she was there she asked a man in the paint department about her peeling paint on the ceiling. He went into a small office and came out with a business card.

"Call this guy," he said. "He specializes in things like that."

With a roll of dimes in hand she found a pay phone and called the City and got the utilities transferred into her name. She called the phone company and they would be out tomorrow to hook the phones back up. She called the garbage service, and also a man her father had done insurance business through, and bought insurance on the building and its contents. So far it had been too easy she thought, but she was spending money like a drunken sailor.

By the end of the next week her apartment above the store was taking shape. A plumber came and fixed the water leak in the basement and set a new stool in her bathroom. The old one was too far-gone to clean. Her bedroom now had new curtains and room darkening shades and a fresh coat of paint. She bought a bedside stand and a new lamp, and also a wardrobe because the room lacked a closet. The kitchen had been repainted white and the cupboards were now clean and full of food and spices. A new toaster, microwave, and coffee pot sat on the counter. The little pine table had a fancy new red and white-checkered tablecloth that made her think of a small café somewhere in Italy. A few pictures and plaques that she had taken from home were hung, and Sears had delivered a new refrigerator, a couch and a matching chair, complete with end tables and lamps. The place was starting to even smell like home.

Jenny piled all of her books and the ones that had been left upstairs along one wall. These would be the last ones she would go through. The men were coming on Monday to sandblast, repair, and repaint the ceiling downstairs in the store. They told her not to bother taking the books off the shelves. They would cover everything, and when they were done they would fix the lights with new bulbs and shields.

There was other good news. Tomorrow she was having lunch with Caroline Finch, and they were going to talk about the business.

It was Saturday and her first full week at her new home and store. She and Caroline would be meeting today at that same little café next door at noon. Jenny had so many questions to ask her and one of the most pressing was why the store seemed to have so few newer books, and so many older ones. Had her dad been a collector? She had said before he was an expert on old books. Jenny had browsed through a few of them and she had a good knowledge herself of what was a rare book. There seemed to be quite a few and why hadn't collectors been called in and the books sold after the store was closed?

Jenny and Caroline could have been taken for mother and daughter. Jenny was dressed in a St. Theresa's sweatshirt and blue jeans, her hair pulled into a ponytail. Caroline on the other hand was impeccably dressed in black slacks with a grey sweater that accented her short gray hair. They sat in a booth next to the window where they could watch the traffic go by.

"I have so many questions to ask you," Jenny said.

"I really hope I can help you," Caroline smiled.

The café was not busy and it was unusually quiet in the place. Both women ordered coffee and salads. For a few minutes they just got acquainted talking about families, and likes and dislikes. Then Jenny reached across and touching Caroline's arm, said, "Tell me about your father and his bookstore."

"What is it you want to know?" she asked.

"Well I noticed when I was going through the inventory that a lot of the books seemed to be old and some of them were quite rare. I wondered if this was some kind of a specialty bookstore and if there was any market for that kind of thing now days."

Caroline seemed nervous twisting her napkin as she talked. "Dad had his own set of customers. People that would come from all over the United States to talk with him and buy and sell books. I often tried to talk him into carrying more of the best sellers, but he always said they were rubbish: Just someone's dirty laundry. He always said that the books he carried were the real writers that had passed the test of time."

"Do you think he would disapprove if I made the store more modern?"

Caroline laughed. "No, it's your store and it's a different world we live in now. But I do hope you keep the rare book trade if you feel you can. It could just be a few shelves someplace in the store. "

"You do know some of these books are worth a lot of money?"

"Yes."---She hesitated for a moment. "Jennifer there's something I want to tell you. I turned down offers for the store that were much larger than yours. They were people who wanted to tear the building down. You were the first one who seemed sincerely interested in keeping it as bookstore and that's what Dad would have wanted. "

Jenny had no comment, except to say "Wow. I had no idea."

"Can I ask you something?" Caroline said.

"Certainly."

"I just lost my job and I was wondering if you were going to need some help running the store."

"I would love to have you," Jenny said. "But right now I'm still weeks from opening and my funds are getting short. Maybe after the store opens and I have some income."

"Let me give you this offer," said Caroline. "I'll work for free until it opens."

Jenny felt like a weight had been lifted from her chest. "Come with me and let me show you want I've done." She glanced at the bill, left some money on the table, and they headed for the bookstore next door.

"Monday the contractor is coming to strip and repaint the ceilings," she exclaimed as they walked inside. All of the shelves and books had been covered with plastic sheeting. "The new lighting is going to be installed and then I need to take all of the books down and refinished the shelves. After that I want to stock some best sellers in about half of the store, and have a special section for the old books. I'll still sell and buy old books, as I do plan on selling a lot of them, and I agree with your dad, they are the real stories that will live for ages. I also believe there's a market for them. Over here-- she pointed to the other side of the store, will be the children's books. "

They walked to the back of the store where the gathering place once existed. "I'm going to put in a self-service coffee bar back here where folks can sit and browse. A plumber is coming to put in a bathroom over there." She pointed to the corner where the back door was now located. "The flooring is going to be replaced with white tile to brighten the place up. Come upstairs and let me show you what I've done."

By the time Caroline said she had to leave, she seemed as excited about the store as Jenny was. They made plans for her to come to work as soon as the contractors were out of there.

Jenny was excited too; a whole new dimension had been added with the addition of Caroline, and she really liked her. That night after work she took a long hot bath and daydreamed in the tub. She allowed herself a second glass of wine that evening, and she was feeling warm inside and out. Things were going well and she seemed less afraid of what the future would bring, and more optimistic about the store. But as she reclined there in the warm soapy water in the tub she had a feeling that something else was still missing in her life. It was something her newfound friendship with Caroline couldn't bring. A feeling that was somewhat sensuous in nature and it had started shortly after her father had passed away. She had never thought of her father in that manner, that would be just sick, but it seemed to be something his absence had brought on. *Why was it suddenly coming on now and where was it coming from?* It was a feeling that seemed to be getting stronger by the day.

Caroline came the week after the contractors left and the two women worked long days getting everything ready for the grand opening. The store was becoming brighter, and more cheerful every day. Jenny found a book supplier who offered to come and help her get the shelves stocked. She was even able to get some of them on consignment. She bought new furniture and some tables and chairs for the back of the store. A coffee vendor came in and set up a coffee machine and a bakery just down the street offered to bring bagels and rolls for her to sell. The new bathroom was nicer than the one she had upstairs. Up front, the window display had new glass and carpeting and a huge banner that said, Watch for grand opening. Jenny bought a new cash register, and all of the bookshelves shined under new coats of stain and varnish.

Caroline brought another color to Jenny's rainbow and the two of them were becoming inseparable. The days were ticking down to the grand opening next week, and both of the women couldn't wait. It had been a lot of work but the finished project could not have turned out better.

Tomorrow a book collector was coming from Minneapolis to look at two rare books she had found hiding amongst the shelves. Caroline had given her a list of potential names to work from, old customers of her dads. The one from Minneapolis had seemed quite enthusiastic about the store opening again. Money was becoming a problem so she hoped he would give her a good offer. She had somewhat of an idea as to their worth from catalogs she had, but the economy was bad right now, and she wasn't sure what the market would bear. Only time would tell.

CHAPTER FIVE

From the day the store opened it became apparent that it was one of the missing attractions in downtown St. Paul, with the exception of the rare books business. Jenny slowly downsized the space she had allotted on the shelves for rare books to just a couple of shelves. Not that she wasn't still interested in it yet-- she was. It just didn't warrant a display area. Her store wasn't that big and the volume of books that were out there that were best sellers, increased each day.

Caroline and Jenny worked so well together and they even hired a couple of college girls to work weekends and evenings. Each morning Jenny would open the store at eight and each evening she could be seen coming down from upstairs to close it up at nine. In between she was in and out as the traffic warranted.

The upstairs became very comfortable and homey with lots of pictures and art on the walls. The living area in the middle of the room was filled with couches, chairs and coffee tables. New appliances in the kitchen gave her ample opportunity to refine her newly found culinary skills. Jenny eventually adapted to the downtown noise and she seldom even heard it anymore. Everything was going great, except there was still this hunger that seemed to exist in her inner being to find someone to settle down with someday. She still missed her dad so much, and he had been the only man in her life. Next week she would be twenty-three years old. She was still an unkissed virgin and she was becoming increasingly worried and sensitive about it. Somewhere, somehow, she knew there was man out there for her, she just didn't know right now, how to attract him.

In one corner of the living room there still existed a stack of books that she had not gone through, and a cardboard box with some old papers in it. Jenny had had good intentions at tackling those few remnants of the old store, but always something would come up and she kept putting it off. But tonight she left the store early and made an old fashioned pot roast for supper. As she ate at the small table her gaze drifted to the books and the box in the corner. For some reason something there was peaking her curiosity, and it wasn't the books.

When she finished eating, Jenny went over to the box, and taking it with her to the couch, started sifting through the pile of musty papers. Most of it seemed to be old newspaper clippings and advertisements from the store from twenty or thirty years ago. There was even a picture of Caroline and her dad, when he was about middle age, and she was a teenager, standing in front of the store. *She sure was a cute kid,* Jenny thought. *I better set this aside and tease her with it tomorrow.* She laughed softly at the thought and continued sorting through the pile.

In the bottom of the box was another box that looked almost like a gift box a dress shirt might come in, wedged in tight. The cover had become almost glued on with age and she worked each corner to get it loose without tearing it. Finally, with it uncovered, she was looking at what appeared to be an old manuscript, yellowed with age. There was no title on the first page, which was largely blank, but down at the bottom was a signature signed in very good penmanship. It simply said, 'G. J. Gildabran.'

Jenny stared at the name for a while. This was not Caroline's father, the man who had owned the store. Who was it? She took the entire manuscript out of the box and laid it on her lap. It appeared to be about a hundred pages or so, all hand written. Although the paper was yellowed, brittle, and in bad shape, the script remained quite bold. As if it had been written recently. It was not bound together, but held together by a small leather cord, through a single eyelet that had been punched in one corner. Thinking she would tear the corner of the paper out if she turned the pages like that, Jenny untied the cord and it fell apart in her fingers. The next page had a heading that said 'Chapter One' and then it was filled with script. She curled her feet under her getting comfortable, intending to read a few pages, but was interrupted by a knock on the door. It was one of the girls from downstairs with a question from a customer about a rare book.

"I'll come down and talk to him," Jenny said. She took the manuscript into her bedroom before she went downstairs, and laid it on the nightstand. She would read it tonight when she went to bed.

It was a stroke of good luck. The man wanted two books from the dwindling supply of rare ones. The catalog had a suggested price of six thousand each and she was sure she would never sell them for that price. They were part of a series and the only two left that the man needed to complete the set, and the only two he could find. He happily paid her the twelve thousand.

She helped the girls close up the store and then retreated upstairs for what she called her quiet time. A warm bath and then she was going to take another look at that manuscript. It had been a good day.

The bath felt wonderful and made her sleepy, or was it the wine. Either way she was feeling very relaxed when she finally slipped between the sheets and picked up the manuscript and started reading.

From the moment Jenny read the first sentence something unexplainable came over her. The ambient noise she had got used to living with disappeared. The humming of the refrigerator in the kitchen, the ticking of her bedside clock, they all seemed to be silenced. It was just her and the story. It was if she was in some kind of hypnotic trance or having an out of body experience she couldn't explain and even more unexplainable, didn't want to. There was no fear or apprehension, just an overwhelming desire to go ahead and read what it said.

Jenny was suddenly aware that the temperature around her had risen considerably, and she was no longer between the clean sheets in her warm nightgown, in her bedroom, but standing on a sandy path next to a rolling farm field that abutted a large forest of mature oak trees. Her clothes felt so strange and different, and looking down she saw she was dressed in clothing that could only be called a frock. She had on black high-buttoned shoes, and lifting her skirts to see them better, she saw that she was wearing frilly petticoats and even farther up, long legged pantaloons for underclothing. Her head was covered with a colorful bonnet that was tied under her chin in a bow and her long hair which had been in a loose braid when she went to bed, was now full of cascading curls, which fell around her shoulders. Where was she, and how did she get here?

For a moment she just took it all in. Not really afraid, just more confused than anything. Then suddenly she heard the whinny of a horse, and looking across the meadow she saw a team of horses hooked to a hay wagon half filled with loose hay. Someone on the far side of the wagon was talking, but she couldn't see who, because of the hay, just a pair of legs under the wagon, going back and forth. She felt vulnerable out in the open on the road, so she walked to the edge of the woods and went back in about fifteen feet deeper into the cover. Finding her way through the trees and brush she walked until she could see the person who was alongside the wagon.

Jennifer stood at the edge of the woods shading her eyes as the team of horses and the man slowly came her way. He appeared not to notice her, but was engrossed in his work that consisted of picking up forks full of hay from windrows that had been formed in the field, and throwing it onto the wagon. He was dressed in long brown loose fitting pants; held up by brown leather suspenders and was wearing a blue work shirt with the sleeves rolled up. His collar was soaked with perspiration as was a patch in the middle of his back. A wide brimmed hat also soaked with sweat was perched on his head.

The man appeared to be in his early thirties with muscular arms that bulged under the fork loads of hay he was lifting. He was deeply tanned and his jaw was square, his sandy hair fell out from under his hat. Already he was close enough to her that she could see his bright blue eyes and hear him talking gently to the horses. They seemed to be getting more nervous by the minute, stomping their feet and tossing their huge heads.

Jenny walked to a stump and sat down. The heat was stifling and she could feel herself getting damp with perspiration, and could feel her dress sticking to her back. For some reason there was no temptation to flee-- she was totally mesmerized by the sight of this man coming towards her.

At last he saw her, and for a moment he just stood there leaning on his fork and smiled at her. Jenny smiled back casually but remained quiet. He took the reins of the horses and walked towards her. When they were about ten feet from her, he dropped the reins and said something to the team that seemed to calm them, then walked slowly over to her where she was still sitting on the stump.

He was handsome in a rugged looking way. He had a warm smile on his face and for some reason, despite the fact that he was a complete stranger-- and she still had no idea how she got here-- or why-- she felt comfortable in his presence.

He offered her his hand and she grasped it, but her gaze never left his face. "I don't believe we've ever met. I'm Garth."

There was something unique about this man. He seemed to be so full of confidence, but at the same time very humble. Her hand felt like a child's in his large hand, hardened with layers of calluses, but yet so warm and comfortable.

"I'm Jennifer," she answered. She offered no other explanations.

"Are you from around here or are just visiting?" he asked.

Jennifer was confused and didn't know how to answer his question. She knew where she was from, but it was almost as if an unseen script was playing out here, and she was not sure her answers would fit the story. "I'm from St. Paul," she finally answered softly.

Garth dropped her hand and squatted down on his haunches in front of her, still sitting on the stump. He cocked his head up, looking at her with a curious smile on his face. He pulled a long blade of grass and placed it in the corner of his mouth.

"St. Paul. That's a long ride," he said. "How'd you get here?"

"I'm not sure," Jenny answered. "But I----" She seemed speechless at the moment. Then quickly composing herself she asked, "Where am I?"

"I think you're where you belong," he answered and chuckled. "Are you thirsty? Come along with me I have some water on the wagon." He stood and took her hand again and they walked to the wagon and the horses through the cut grass stubble. She could smell the huge animals as she passed by them but they remained docile and seemingly undisturbed by her.

Garth reached under the hay and pulled out a mason jar wrapped in a towel. He unscrewed the lid and handed the jar to her. "It might be a bit warm," he said, "but it's wet."

Jenney suddenly realized she was parched and tipped the jar up and drank. The water was refreshing, and all the while she drank she couldn't take her eyes off this man. What was happening here and why was she not afraid? It was a dream she thought. It had to be.

"I can finished this haying later," he said. "Would you walk with the horses and me to the pasture? They need to rest and drink themselves. It's not that far, just over the rise." He pointed to the right and she could see some buildings hid in the trees.

She wanted to say no, I have to go, but that's what she had always said when men had tried to befriend her. This was so different this time, and she had no idea where she would go anyway, not knowing where she was. She knew she was here for a reason, but still had no idea what it could be.

Jenny watched as he unhitched the horses and took off the rigging and tacking. Then he took the reins and splitting them, handed her one set. "That's Josie," he said, nodding at the mare Jenny was leading. "This one here is Adam. I'd be lost without them."

They walked slowly toward the house and the barn, the two horses plodding along behind them. They came to a fence and Garth stopped to unhook the gate. He slipped off the rest of the reins and tack and the two horses walked slowly away. For a second they stood silently watching the big animals as they drank from the stock tank.

"Can I show you around?" Garth asked. She nodded and they walked toward the house.

Jenny awakened startled. She could once more hear the clock ticking and the traffic outside. The dream had been so vivid, so real, and now she was shaking. She looked down into her lap and she noticed that Chapter Two was now the next page showing. On her right were five pages all turned upside down in a neat stack. Had she been reading while she was dreaming?

Jenny's hand went to the hair on the back of her neck. It was damp, as if she had been sweating; yet it was cool in the bedroom. Was she sick? Her hand went to her forehead. She wasn't that warm.

She picked up the pages she had read and tried to read them again, but nothing happened. It was just her reading the script. Then a vision of Garth came to her and she felt sad and confused. Who was that man and how could she see him again?

CHAPTER SIX

Caroline was at the store bright and early the next morning. They received an order last week that they hadn't unpacked yet, and she was anxious to get the books priced and on the shelves before the store opened. She was sitting on the floor buried in boxes and piles of books when Jenny came downstairs.

Today was also the day the St. Paul Chamber of Commerce was stopping by to interview Jenny for an upcoming article they were going to write about, on the store reopening. Jenny wore a nice white sweater and blue skirt instead of the typical jeans and sweatshirt she usually wore. She had some makeup on too, which was unusual, and small gold hoop earrings.

"Wow look at the boss," Caroline said. "You got a man coming around or something?"

Jenny laughed. "I wish," she said.

Caroline knew Jenny had never dated or had any kind of a serious relationship with a man. They talked about it on more than one occasion. "You're a pretty girl Jenny, and a nice one. Most men would trip over each other trying to get your attention. How have you stayed out of the dating game so long?"

"I don't know Caroline. I just guess my mind has never really wrapped around the issue. Maybe I've been too busy going to school, and now too busy with this store. We do have visitors coming today from the Chamber and they are going to feature our store in next month's magazine. I guess I just wanted to look nice for them." *Anything to change the subject,* she thought.

Jenny looked around at the store as the two women worked. When she first saw this place it had been a dark dungeon of filth and mold, but now it was radiant with in its new lights and colorful displays and shelves. The coffee area in the back had been an overwhelming success and the good smells that came from it had dissipated all of the foul odors from the past. She was so proud of what had been accomplished in so little time. She was doubly fond of her new relationship with Caroline and what she had brought into her life. The store was making money now. More money than she thought it would ever make, and she made a mental note to give Caroline a raise from what they had agreed on when they started.

As they worked shoulder to shoulder unwrapping and pricing books Jenny's mind was not on her disappointing love life. Instead it was on the dream last night, that she couldn't get out of her mind no matter how hard she tried. She could still picture this Garth as if she had known him forever. She could still feel the summers heat and the smell of the horses. But it was something Garth had said that really haunted her. She remembering asking him in the dream where was she, and he had answered, "You are where you belong." What did he mean by that? She looked up at the clock, it was five to nine. Time to open the store.

As the day went on Jenny continued to be preoccupied with the dream and the more she thought about it, the more questions she had. Had this been a one-time shot? Had it been just that, a quirky dream from the mind of a love starved woman, who had long thought about a relationship with a man, and never had acted seriously about having one. But the more she tried to discount it as just a dream, the stronger it became and somehow she felt there had to be more to it than that.

The people from the Chamber of Commerce were very kind, and they brought her a plaque to hang in the store and took lots of pictures of the store and Jenny, and a young man named Willard who could have played a nerd in any movie to the tee. Willard interviewed her in length about her plans for the future and what made her revive this ageing store.

For Jenny the visit from this organization was a shot in the arm that went beyond her wildest expectations. Surely she could use the advertisement, but to be accepted into the business community of downtown St. Paul, well, this was simply a dream come true.

The Magic Book

The rest of the day flew by and before she knew it, Caroline was putting on her coat, and the evening girls were there to take over. Jenny's mind had settled down a little bit from this morning, but as soon as everyone left, she hurried upstairs after locking up for the night. Her thoughts went right back to the manuscript.

She didn't linger in the tub as long tonight. She was too anxious to read the next chapter. In fact she had been anxious to read it last night, but for some reason something told her not to go on with it right then. That she needed to digest what she had read before she went on reading another chapter.

She crawled between the sheets and adjusted her reading lamp. Then taking a deep breath she reached for the story. She had hoped all day that the same thing that happened last night would happen, when she read again, but now that the time was here it was a little scary. She had no idea what was going to happen to her, but she settled down and something told her to just play along, and it would all be worth while. She remembered last night when she tried to start the story over, the magic wasn't there. Would tonight be any different? She picked up page one of Chapter Two.

Jenny never felt it coming on. For brief moment it was unusually quiet again and then the next thing she knew she was back walking with Garth across the yard to the house.

The house was a simple one-story home with a back porch that was enclosed, and a front porch that was open. It had wood shake shingles and clapboard siding that had never been painted and now it was weathered gray.

"I built the house and the barn with lumber from the land I cleared. We worked so hard for a few years it seemed we hardly had time for each other."

"We?" Jennifer asked.

"Yes my wife and I. She passed away two years ago in childbirth."

"I'm so sorry," Jenny said.

Garth shrugged his shoulders. "It was hard for a while, trying to keep the place going and taking care of my son." They had reached the house and were now standing on the top step. Garth held the screen door open for her and motioned for her to go inside.

She saw no evidence of anyone else around and thought she would wait until they got inside to address the issue of the boy.

"I have some bread that is rising and some fresh honey. If you don't mind waiting while I build a fire and warm up the oven, we can have some fresh bread."

Jenny looked around the sparsely furnished kitchen. A large kitchen stove sat at one end and a crooked round table sat in the middle with two chairs. Another matching chair sat against the far wall. There were some dishes stacked on shelves but no cupboards. Two brass laundry tubs were in one corner behind the door.

"I would love some fresh bread," she said.

"Sit down please," Garth said, and pulled one of the chairs out for her.

There was a dish on the table with what she thought was butter in it. It was more white than yellow. A jar of jelly, and bowl of honey also sat on the table. The checkered oilcloth was worn and tattered, but clean. Across from Jenny was a newspaper folded over.

"You get the newspaper way out here?" she asked.

"No. This was a gift from a friend of mine. It's the paper from New York the day the Titanic hit the iceberg and sunk. It's been over six years since that terrible tragedy. I just keep it as a souvenir."

Jenny reached across and picked up the paper while Garth was getting his bread in the oven. She had read the story many times in history books but it wasn't the story that caught her eye, it was the date. April 12th, 1912. Garth had said it was almost five years ago. My God, she had gone backwards in time almost fifty-six years. How was this possible?

Garth came over and sat down across from her.

"Are you staying close by?" he asked.

She didn't know how to answer, but at last she said, "For now."

She wanted to find out more about him so she quickly changed the subject from her to him. "You mentioned your boy."

"Yes. Josh. He's four right now and staying with my wife's parents while I get the crops in. In the winter he stays with them too when the bad weather comes. I do miss him a lot, but until he gets older they will have him. It's better this way. I try to ride over there every week or so to see them, but it's a four hour ride."

"Where do you wife's folks live?"

"In St. James," he answered. "It's east of here, and north of Mankato. Her father is an Attorney there."

She nodded her head to acknowledge she understood. That's all she understood right now. But as strange as this whole thing was, she was becoming more fascinated with Garth by the minute and cared less about how or why.

"How did your wife die?" Jenny asked. "Oh that's right, you said she died giving birth. Maybe don't you want to talk about it."

"No that's fine," he said. "She did die in childbirth. Something went terribly wrong and she bled to death. The baby only lived a few hours."

"Did the doctor say what went wrong?"

Garth looked at her quizzically. "There was no doctor, Jennifer, only me."

Jennifer didn't know what to say so she just hung her head.

Garth sensed she was uncomfortable so he said. "Let's walk outside while we're waiting for the bread to bake. It's getting warm in here anyway with the oven going."

It was getting later in the day and the heat of the day outside was dissipating. The grass was high, but he took her to a flower garden that was in bloom and they cut some flowers for the house. She was thirsty so he primed the pump and he held her hair for her while she drank from the mouth of the pump by cupping her hand under it and slurping out of her hand. The water was cold and refreshing. When she stood up Garth wiped her chin with the back of his hand, and then dried his hand on his shirt. His touch had been so delicate she was amazed. No man had ever done that for her before, but then she had never drunk water in this way before either.

They went to the barn and she saw the three cows and two calves grazing behind the barn in a small pasture. Chickens scurried everywhere in the barnyard looking for a dropped kernel of corn to eat. The two horses she had met earlier stood by the barn door, as if waiting to go finish the day's work.

From out of nowhere came a small Collie-type dog waging its tail but keeping its distance. "He's friendly but extremely shy," Garth laughed.

They walked over to the garden and Garth pointed out all of the vegetables and fruit trees. "Don't look at the weeds," he said. "That's a never ending job."

Then Jenny saw the wooden cross next to the garden. On it was inscribed: Priscilla and baby. Born Jan. 20, 1890 died Nov. 3rd 1916. Jenny walked over and ran her hand over the letters but quickly jerked it away with a sliver in her palm.

"Get stuck?" Garth asked.

"No I'm fine," Jenny said, somewhat embarrassed, and put her hand in her pocket so he couldn't see it.

They stood by the graveside for a moment but Garth didn't seem to want to be there, so he said, "I think that breads about done." They walked back to the house.

"Not like Priscilla made, but it is her recipe," he said as he cut the fresh bread. "I always get it burnt on the outside and doughy in the middle. You know Jennifer tomorrow starts the County Fair. Its just about an hours ride if you would like to go."

The noise of the city and her apartment was back and she was wide-awake holding the last page of Chapter Two of the manuscript. All of the other pages were turned over beside her, just like last night. Jenny didn't know what to think. It was a dream, it had to be, but it was so real she could swear it had actually happened. She gathered up the pages and put them back in a pile. She was suddenly thirsty and her hand hurt. Looking down she saw that somehow, somewhere, she had picked up a sliver.

CHAPTER SEVEN

Jenny stood in front of the vanity with a tweezers trying to get a hold of the sliver of wood in her hand. She could be a big baby when it came to things like this. She remembered all of the times her father had bandaged her 'owies,' as she called them when she had been a child, and put a Mickey Mouse band-aid on them.

The funny thing about this one was, she had no idea where she had picked it up. She didn't remember it when she took her bath. At last she got a firm hold on the little piece of wood and it came out in one piece. It was not the color of any kind of wood she remembered from the store. She shuttered as she poured some peroxide over the wound and watched it fizzle. She seemed more tired than usual and bed would feel good.

As she lay in bed trying to collect her thoughts, Garth once again came to the forefront. She had dreamt of him again tonight in the story and why had she slipped away like that once more when she read the story? It was almost like the script itself put her into some kind of a trance and that was scary. What if she didn't come back out of it? She had on many occasions read books half the night, and never before fallen asleep or got that involved in them. Garth seemed so real to her as if she knew him better than her mind was letting onto. Like the night before she noticed that she could only recall bits and pieces of the dream she seemed to be living. She had no trouble remembering Garth, but the rest of it was just outside of her depth of recall. She had a hint of an old house and some farm animals and something about a wooden cross. Why was that important?

She picked up the pages of Chapter Two again and started rereading them but nothing happened, and the story had little to do with what she remembered. It was as if there was another story, within the story that wasn't written, but it took the written story to take her back to 1918. Jenny looked at Chapter Three but something told her, don't go there. Not tonight anyway. She was still somewhat shaken.

The next day was Saturday and Caroline's day off. The two college girls, Amy and Angie, would split the day working with Jenny. It had snowed the night before and for some reason, most likely the weather, traffic was light and subsequently so was business. By early afternoon she asked Angie if she thought she could handle things by herself for a while.

"No problem," Angie said.

Jenny put on her warmest coat and the stocking hat she'd worn for many years. Although it had snowed five or six inches it was still reasonably warm outside and she wanted some fresh air, and a new environment. She walked up St. Peter Street to the next cross street and then started walking towards the Summit Hill district: A long wide street filled with historic mansions that sat high up on a bluff that overlooked the city. It was quite a hike but about an hour later she stood at a small scenic over-look that looked down on the sprawling city below her. She cleaned the snow off a bench that had been put there, maybe for just that reason, and sat down to think.

She thought about her dad again and soon a few tears filled her eyes but she quickly wiped them away. She hadn't come here for that she thought. Something else had brought her here and it was very confusing. It had to do with her feelings for men in general. Maybe she should make a better effort to put herself out there where she could meet someone. She could join a health club or a church maybe, anything to be more sociable. It was just too lonely living life like this. For a long time she had always had a reason, or more accurately an excuse to be by herself. Yes, there was a difference between her dreams and reality. One of them was life in general, and the other was just an escape from reality.

Then she thought about the man in the dream again. *Garth, he had said his name was. Why did she remember his name and nothing else from the dream? Was this Gods way of telling her it was time to look for a mate?*

The Magic Book

It was getting dark when she got back to the store. It had felt so invigorating to be outside again but her mind was still as confused as before.

"Angie how was business?" she asked as she brushed out her hair after removing her cap.

"Not much happening." Angie said. "I did sell a women some Dr. Seuss books. Anything to keep the little rug rats occupied, she told me." Angie laughed.

Jenny smiled and then yawned. She was tired. "I think I'll go upstairs for the rest of the day if you're alright. Lock up behind you."

"Sounds good."

It was only five p.m. but Jenny was restless. She wanted to get back to the story and her dream. Yes she had fears about what was happening, but she had made the decision to get to the bottom of it. Right now she had to make supper and balance out the books. They closed at six on Saturdays, so Angie would be up soon with the day's receipts.

She warmed up some leftover beef stew from last night and sliced a couple of pieces of French bread. It tasted good--- she had worked up quite an appetite outside on her walk.

Angie was there right at six and Jenny took the bag from her. "What have you got going tonight girl?" she asked her young employee.

"Oh I'll probably just go over to my boyfriend's place and hang out. Maybe watch some T.V. He's always broke so outside of playing around with each other, there's nothing much else to do that's free." She smiled looking a little embarrassed at what she had said.

Jenny laughed and said, "Have a great night," and went and sat back down at the table. The weeks receipts, minus wages and expenses, still left her over seven hundred dollars. *Not bad for this time of the year,* she thought.

Then she thought about what Angie had said. What she wouldn't give to have someone from the opposite sex to talk to tonight. What a comfortable feeling it must be to belong to someone.

It was time to take a bath. Tonight before she stepped into the tub she took a moment to look at her nude body in the mirror on the back of the door. *I look good,* she thought. *My breasts aren't big but they are more than just a little adequate.* She felt one of her breasts and wondered what it would feel like to have someone else fondle them.

In the tub the water enveloped and calmed her. She always left the hot water running a little to keep the bathwater warm. *Someday I'll have a big tub with lots of hot water and those bubbly jets,* she thought.

Snug in her flannel nightgown she crawled into bed and somewhat apprehensively reached for the manuscript. Was she ready for this she wondered? She picked up Chapter Three.

In the time it took to read the first sentence, it happened again and she was back outside of Garth's farmhouse. He was slowly walking the surrey and the horse up from the barn. Josie was nervous and throwing her head from side to side. She seemed more than ready to go, filled with nervous energy.

Jenny's dress was different than the first two times she had been here. This one was green with a strip of white starched lace around the high neckline that itched and felt uncomfortable. The sleeves buttoned at the wrists and the bodice was tight, as was the waist, so tight it felt restrictive and made it hard to breathe.

She had on different bonnet than she'd worn before too -- dark green, and in her hand was a small brightly colored parasol.

Garth clicked his tongue and held back on the reins. "Whoa Josie," he said.

"Jennifer, you're beautiful. I feel so lucky to have you accompanying me." His smile echoed his words. He reached for her waist and with one hand on each side lifted her and placed her on the surrey seat as if she were a mere child. "Someday I might be able to afford a motor car," he said. "They're getting pretty popular."

It was a beautiful day and the clopping of Josie's hoofs on the packed road seemed to be all Jenny wanted to listen to as the surrey bumped from side to side. She knew where she had come from when Garth had asked her the other day, but she was unable to make any comparisons from the world where she lived in her real life, to the one she was in now. It was almost as if it didn't exist and she was unable to go back to her world when she was in Garth's world. Likewise she was unable to go to Garths world without the story. It was all too confusing.

Suddenly the surrey wheels hit a deep rut and the carriage lurched to the left. She felt Garth's strong arm encircle her waist and hold her to the seat next to him. She moved over until their shoulders were touching. It wasn't just to be safer; she wanted to be closer to this man.

The path they had been on suddenly widened and they were on a very sandy, but much wider road and other carriages could be seen heading in the same direction. "It looks like we're not the only ones heading to the fair," Garth said, and urged Josie into a slightly faster pace.

From the much-improved road they had been on, they now turned onto an even better and wider gravel road, and now motorcars passed by them, their noisy gasoline engines startling the horse. Garth had to take charge of the reins he had held loosely in his hand to keep Josie in check. Still he yearned for the day he would have one of those horseless carriages.

At last Jenny could see the buildings of the city, and Garth turned down a short cobblestone street and through a wide gate into the fair grounds. As soon as they stopped, a couple of young men took the surrey and Josie away to care for them.

As they walked to the main buildings Jennifer marveled at the colorful stands that were set up along the side of the road and also at how large the crowd was.

There were people selling their homemade wares, and vegetables: Baked goods, jelly and jams, and canned fruit. There were leather shops, and blacksmiths, and a man selling a cure-all for almost anything that ailed you. Garth bought some cinnamon bread and some lemonade and they stopped to spread a blanket on the grassy ground while they ate and rested.

"Do you get lonely out in the country living like you do?" Jenny asked.

"I do," he said, "but I'm so busy most of the time that I never have time to think about it. It isn't often I get to town or do things like this. You hate to go by yourself. Running into you has made this time very special for me."

Jenny blushed, but deep down her mind wanted to echo the words.

Refreshed, they went to the livestock buildings and looked at the animals. Jenny saw a live birth of a foal and she was fascinated at the miracle of life. Just minutes after delivery the baby horse was trying out its legs and nursing.

Garth wanted to see the steam tractors so they stopped and watched the big machines belching smoke and white clouds of steam, pulling loads of rocks several teams of horses would have trouble with. It was amazing what the world had come to. In late afternoon they watched a roping and riding exhibition and listened to a band concert, but with darkness falling Garth said, "I think it best we call it a day." They ate a supper of baked chicken and biscuits at a church stand and then the same two young men, who had taken the surrey and Josie away, brought them back and they were on their way home.

They seemed to be in less of a hurry on the way home and the horse sensed it too, walking way below her usual trot. The evening had started out warm, with a moon that was full, but as the night took over from the dusk, there was just a hint of the colder weather that would be coming in the not to distance future. Shucks of corn illuminated by moonlight stood like silent sentinels in the fields as they rode by.

Gradually the road narrowed again and again, and soon they were back on the mostly grassy path that would take them home to the farm. Garth didn't hold her waist as he did on the way to the fair to steady her, but this time he rode with his arm around her holding her into his side, her head on his shoulder. She had wrapped a blanket around her shoulders for added warmth but she could feel the heat of his body also. When they finally pulled up to the house her head was still on his broad shoulder and her hand was holding his. His long hair tickled her face and she could smell his masculine scent.

"This was wonderful day for me Jennifer," Garth said finally releasing his arm from around her. "I want to thank you for coming with me," he said, as Josie stopped and snorted loudly.

Garth reached down and tipped her sleepy face up to his and he pushed her bonnet back and kissed her gently on the forehead. Then he got down, and walking around picked her by the waist once more and set her on the ground. She watched as he led the horse and surrey back to the barn to put them away. It was at this time she sensed something strange was happening to her, and her feelings for this man.

The Magic Book

Jenny was startled when she awakened this time. For a second she wasn't sure where she was, and then she heard a bus go by out on the street. She had to go to the bathroom, and she was chilled. She went into the bathroom and tried to digest what she could remember from the dream, but once again she could only remember Garth. This time she did remember that he'd kissed her. Finished relieving herself she turned on the light and looked in the mirror, as her face felt unusually sore. Jenny could only gasp. Her cheeks looked burned from sun or wind, and there was a piece of straw stuck in her hair.

Back in the bedroom once again, the pages of the chapter she had been reading were turned over and stacked neatly in a pile. The page showing now was Chapter four. This time she didn't even try rereading what she had been reading in her dream. She knew it wouldn't take her back there, because it wasn't the same story, and she knew Chapter Four had to wait for another time.

CHAPTER EIGHT

It was Sunday and the bookstore was closed. Sunday was the day she usually cleaned and stocked the store. Not that it didn't get cleaned every day, but this was the day the mop buckets and dust rags came out and everything got that real deep cleaning. Maybe someday she would be rich enough to hire some people to come in and do the cleaning and she could truly have the day off.

Jenny sat at her small kitchen table and nursed her coffee and picked at a piece of day old coffee cake. She had come so far in just a few months and she was happy about that, but today she was troubled about something that was going on in her mind. She was obsessed with Garth, whatever his name was. *Yes,* she thought, *how strange it was that she didn't even know his last name. Maybe the next time she went there she was going to have to ask him, that is, if she could remember to ask him.*

She warmed up her coffee and pulled her robe tighter around her. It felt chilly in here this morning,.

This whole experience she was going through was unnerving. It was like walking through a strange house you had never been in and discovering wonderful things with each door you opened and each crook and cranny you looked in. In real life you would have fear telling you that you might end up somewhere you don't want to be, but this was not real life and somewhere, somehow, there was a secret here about Garth that was begging to be discovered, and she had come to far not to know the rest of the story. She had to know what really was going to happen, or had happened with her and Garth, even though she understood, she had no power to change the story. She shivered. It was time to get dressed and get to work.

By early afternoon the store was clean, and Jenny was tired, but not too tired to want to get out of the store for while. She changed her clothes and decided to go to a movie downtown. It had been a long time since she had done anything for herself.

The theater was only a few blocks away and the feature was starting in just a few minutes. The movie was 'The Godfather' starring Marlon Brando. Not exactly what she was looking for, but a good way to kill the afternoon all the same. She stayed close to the back of the theater in case she wanted to leave early without disturbing others. Directly in front of her sat a man and woman in their late twenties and it was obvious they cared deeply about each other. Not in a promiscuous, showy way, but just the way she smiled and seemed to hang on his every word. He in-turn seemed to be infatuated with her, touching her hair and face as he talked and looking deeply into her eyes as if they were the only two people in the theater. The light dimmed and the movie started.

Jenny was interested in the movie only because she was a great Brando fan. She had loved him in, 'In The Water Front.' As good as this film was, she couldn't resist stealing glances at the couple from time to time. That's what she needed in her life, someone who would love her, and share her life with her. Right now she had many good friends, but no one to fill that void except for a man who could only be explained as a figment of her imagination. Suddenly she became emotional and knew she had to leave or risk becoming a spectacle.

She walked down along the riverfront to a park and sat watching the fog coming off the cold water. The city seemed to nap a little on Sunday afternoons like its citizens. That's what she should have been doing, curling up with a good book. Her attention span was shot right now and that was not conducive to enjoying a book, or anything else for that matter. Maybe her biggest problem was she knew what she wanted but she didn't know how to get it. She needed a mother to talk to like most daughters had, but that was out of the question, or was it? A thought came to her that maybe now would be a good time to talk with Caroline about something other than books, and business, and it wasn't going to wait until tomorrow.

Jenny went back and got her car started, She knew where Caroline lived. It was to far to walk, and almost to short to drive, but maybe she would just drop in and see if she had time to talk. She could use that raise she wanted to give Caroline as an excuse for stopping by. If her friend was busy, she would just leave.

She knew Caroline's husband traveled a lot for his business and maybe, just maybe, she too was alone this afternoon. Then again maybe she wasn't even home.

Dusk was falling as she pulled up in front of the house. She could see a light on in the big front window, so she parked and shut the car off. Either she was going to find some help, or make fool out of herself, but she was determined to do this.

From the time Jenny and Caroline sat down it seemed as if the stage was set for this conversation. Caroline's husband was not home, and she too was spending a lonely Sunday afternoon. Over coffee and cookies they talked about the store and how well it had done. It was then that Jenny told Caroline, "I want to pay you more money. You've become extremely important to me and the store, and you're big part of its success."

Caroline was touched but she told Jenny, "No I don't want more money. I just want to see the store succeed."

"I insist," Jenny said. "It will be on your check next week."

"I won't cash it," she replied. "Lets talk about something else."

"Tell me about how you met your husband," Jenny said. "I'm not being nosey, I need to get educated, or I fear I'm going to be a ugly wrinkled old maid."

Caroline laughed and said, "Nonsense. My husband and I have had a long and good marriage. We've raised three children and we still like to spend time with each other. But there were dark days too, and you have to accept that as part of life. No marriage is perfect and no man is perfect. You're a pretty girl with so much to offer and I'm sure that your prince charming is just around the corner."

Jenny smiled and touched Caroline's hand as if to say thanks. *She wanted so badly to share her dream story, but she knew it was so unbelievable, even Caroline would think she had lost her mind. Maybe when she was done reading the manuscript, she would share it with her but she knew it wouldn't make sense because the dream she was having had little to do with the story itself. Maybe it was a bad idea anyway you looked at it.*

They talked some more about the store and Caroline gave her some new ideas she had had on advertising. Her ideas always made sense.

The Magic Book

At last Jenny sensed it was time to leave. She had no good reason to go home right now, or maybe she did have a reason, and he was called Garth.

Aunt Rita called shortly after she got home and Jenny talked with her for a while and then begged off saying that she had a lot of work to do. She hung up and went in and ran her bath water.

As she got into bed Jenny was once again filled with apprehension. Where would the story take her tonight? She carefully arranged the pages and then picked up page one of Chapter four. The magical transformation came once more.

When she had last left Garth he had been putting the horse and carriage away. Now he was coming back from the barn and this time he was in his Sunday best. He wore a white shirt with a dangling string bow tie. Over this was a black vest and a matching suit jacket and pants. He clucked his tongue softly at Josie as he approached. Jenny noticed that her dress was different then the one she had last worn the day they went to the fair. Why could she remember this from dream to dream but she had no recollection of her clothing when she was awake?

There was snow on the ground and it was much colder than the last time. Clearly months had passed since their last meeting.

Garth smiled as he approached her. "We better get going," he said. "Its about a half hour ride to the church. I'll go get Josh." He stepped by her and went into the house. When he came back out he was carrying a small boy half wrapped in a quilt. "Josh, this is Jennifer. You remember I told you about her." Josh nodded his head, full of sandy blond curls. He looked at her with shyness, half hiding his face in his hands. Garth put him up on the seat and then lifted Jennifer by the waist as he always did, and set her beside him.

"How long is Josh staying?" Jennifer asked.

"Oh, a couple of weeks. There's not a lot going on right now around the farm so I have time to care for him. He comes down to the barn in the mornings when I milk the cows, and helps me feed the chickens and geese."

Jenny held the small boy to her side but his eyes were on his father. "Thanksgiving came early this year," Garth said. "I mean, I know it's the same date as always, but this year it seems like summer and fall just ran together."

Jenny and Josh seemed to hit it off, each telling silly jokes on the way to the church, and Garth looked over and smiled at both of them.

The church was small and sat on a hillside nestled in some tall pine trees. It had a white steeple with a cross on top and already there were many carriages tied up alongside of it. Garth carried Josh once more, but his right hand found Jennifer's and they walked to a small sanctuary where Garth left his hat on a shelf. She had never seen him before without it, and his long brown hair fell almost to his shoulders.

Inside the Vicar smiled and talked to Jennifer as if he had always known her, while welcoming all three of them to the service. He was old and rotund, dressed in the frocks of his trade, holding a bible to his chest as he talked. She took his hand limply and remarked, "How nice it is to be here again." The words stuck in her throat. Why had she said it? Had she been here before? They sat close to the back on wooden pews that were very straight backed and hard. An old woman at the front pumped her legs up and down to fill the organ bellows with the air that carried out the music she was playing. She bobbed her head with every note and sang along with the congregation.

Then it was quiet and the old Pastor took his place behind a small pulpit, cleared his throat, and began to speak. "Today," he said, "we come before Almighty God to give thanks on this Thanksgiving Day. Let us bow our heads in prayer."

His sermon was long and fiery but soon the last hymn had been sung and they were standing outside. Garth talked with several of the men, mostly about the war. The United States had declared war on Germany this spring and it seemed that it was starting to touch everyone. Garth seemed to take it very seriously.

On the ride home Jennifer asked Garth about the war, as she didn't seem to know a lot about it. He would only shake his head sadly, and said, "Its something we need to take very seriously."

Once in the warm house Garth tended the stove and the goose he had in the oven. Jenny made wild rice dressing that somehow she knew how to make. She ground cranberries in a grinder and cooked them on top of the stove, standing side by side with this man she was so fascinated with. Josh played on the floor with a box of toys that Garth had brought into the kitchen. Jenny stole a glance from time to time at the rest of the house, but she never left the kitchen that day.

Josh fell asleep in Jenny's arms after dinner while playing with some small wooden soldiers on the table top and Garth came and took him and brought him into the other room. When he came back he walked to her and took her into his arms. No words were said but she could feel the need in her body to know more about this man. He reached down and lifted her chin and kissed her softly on the lips. "Thank you for a wonderful Thanksgiving," he whispered and kissed her briefly one more time.

When Jenny awoke this time she was sitting up and holding a pillow to her bosom. She ran her fingertips across her lips. He had kissed her, and that was all she remembered, except for a fleeting memory of a small boy that looked so much like his father.

In her lap was the rest of Chapter Four, tuned over as always. She stacked the pages on the nightstand with the others she had read, and the four she hadn't yet. This whole dream had been so real, so vivid that it left her emotionally spent. What did it mean and where was it taking her?

Suddenly she was aware of something in her still clutched hand that was holding the pillow. Jenny opened up her hand and there was a small wooden soldier. She buried her head in the pillow and sobbed.

CHAPTER NINE

On Monday morning Jenny opened the store, but when Caroline showed up she said, "I'm going upstairs for a while. I guess I caught a bug or something, I'm just not feeling very well."

Caroline came over and put her hand on Jenny's forehead. "You do feel a little warm," she said. "Go lie down for a while and maybe take some aspirin."

She hated to lie to Caroline but she was just too mixed up to think straight right now. She had lain awake half the night thinking about Garth and his son. This whole story was so bizarre it was getting creepy. She went upstairs and laid down on her couch, deep in thought.

There was something terribly strange going on with this manuscript and this incredible dream. Everybody had dreams from time to time, but no one had an ongoing dream four times in four nights. This whole thing was a continuation of sorts of the story of this man's life, back in a period she knew little about, and she had no idea where it was taking her. Maybe it was time to throw the whole thing away and get back to reality. What good could come from this except to make her more confused, and more misled about her failure to find a man in her life? You couldn't fall in love with a ghost.

Jenny went to the table and poured herself some coffee. All of her life she had always been good about rationalizing and listening to both sides of any issue. Never had she been one to jump to conclusions. *On the other hand she had only been through part of this incredible story. Was it trying to tell her there was another part? She wouldn't know until she finished the story, would she? It wasn't a trip she wanted to take, but it was a trip she had to take, or spend the rest of her life wondering what might have been. Maybe she just had to lighten up and not let it destroy her.*

"You feeling better?" Caroline asked, as Jenny came back down to the store later in the day.

"Yes, much better thank you. I have a meeting tonight with some people who want me to be on the library board, so maybe it was just nerves about that, that had me so upset, I don't know."

Caroline came and put her hand on Jenny's. "You'll do just fine," she said. Around suppertime Jenny went upstairs to clean up for her meeting that would be held over at the Government Center. She knew it was to her advantage to rub elbows with all of the people in the community; after all she was a businesswomen now.

The meeting was brief and Jenny told the other members of the board she would be honored to be a part of the system. Books were her forte and what she had studied for so hard in college. It fit right in with the library boards objective. They were impressed with her and told her they would be in touch and soon.

It had been along day and she was especially weary when she got ready for bed that night. She walked to the bathroom for her usual bath, but tonight it was going to be brief: No candles, no lingering daydreams or lounging in the soapy water.

She gave some thought about skipping the next chapter tonight as she climbed into bed. Maybe it was fear that was making her so apprehensive about reading on, and what it might do to her mind. No, she reasoned, she had been through that thought process earlier today. She had to read the rest of the manuscript and she really didn't have a choice. She picked up Chapter Five.

It was Christmas Eve as Jennifer came on the scene. It was the first time she had been in the living room of the house. Against one wall a parlor stove crackled from the fire within its belly and she could feel the heat radiating out into the room. There was a large window in the room made out of many small panes of glass in it. The frost was thick on the glass and it was hard to see outside, but what she could see showed huge snow banks and a frozen landscape. She shivered and pulled the shawl she was wearing tighter around her shoulders.

There was a couch and two chairs in the room but she was sitting on the wood plank floor on a blanket, next to a pine Christmas tree with a smattering of homemade decorations. Several candles and one oil lantern was burning, offering their meager light to the occasion. Sitting in her lap was little Josh, looking at a cloth book she had been reading to him. He seemed to be comfortable and at peace with her, as if they had been together many times. His bright blue eyes flickered in the light of the candles. His tiny hands held the edges of the book until the page was finished, and then he would turn the page and look up at her.

Behind her was a doorway with a curtain drawn across it. *It had to be his bedroom* she thought. Also behind her, but above her, was a loft and she could see the edge of a made up bed. Just then the back door banged open and Garth walked into the room wearing a worn sheepskin jacket, with a bent arm filled with wood for the stove. There was frost on his eyebrows and his cheeks were red and ruddy. He smiled widely as he dropped the wood into the wood box and coming over to her knelt down in front of her. He jostled Josh's hair and then taking Jennifer's cheeks into those cold rough hands he said. "Merry Christmas sweetheart."

They had dishes of plum pudding and some venison chips that Garth had dried. As the evening drew to a close, Garth said it was time to open gifts. Josh's eyes lit up when his dad said he had a special gift for him. He went into his bedroom and after a brief delay, came out with a wagon. The wheels were steel but they were covered with rubber. The box was made of steel and Garth had added wooden sides to it. Inside the wagon were two more gifts, one that was for Josh, and he opened it with anticipation. It was a wooden horse and carriage from his grandparents. The other gift was a warm knitted scarf for Garth from his in-laws. Garth stood up so he could reach into his watch pocket. He brought out a small silver chain with a delicate locket on it. "This was from my mother," he said. "She gave it to me after my wife died and I hoped you would wear it."

He leaned over, and lifting Jennifer's long hair, fastened the clasp behind her while he kissed her softly on the back of her neck.

"I feel so bad," Jennifer said. "I have nothing to give to you."

"Just give me your love," Garth whispered.

The Magic Book

Long after Josh had been put to bed they sat at the kitchen table and talked. They talked about the weather and the economy, but eventually the conversation came back to the war. "If it wasn't for Josh I would join the army and go fight for my country," Garth said. "The war is going badly overseas. Many of the men are dying from tuberculosis and mustard gas. Each time I get to town the news is worse."

Jennifer could sense his deep concern, but right now she didn't know what to do for him. She went around the table and took him into her arms. She could feel the hardness of his body from long days in the fields. She had never felt more secure in her life than she did right now in his arms. They kissed, tenderly at first, but then more lingering kisses. She wanted him so badly but she sensed the time was still not right.

When she awoke the alarm clock said seven thirty-five. She had overslept and the store opened in ten minutes! She pulled on some underwear, knee socks, jeans, and a white cardigan sweater and then ran into the bathroom to brush her teeth. How could she have forgotten to set the clock, and on the one day Caroline was not coming in until noon.

For a minute she was too preoccupied and angry at herself to think about last nights dream, but then looking up at herself in the mirror she caught a glimpse of silver and saw the chain and locket.

She sat down on the toilet stool and let the chain slide through her fingers until she came to the locket. Carefully she opened it, but it was empty.

Jenny put the locket in the same envelope with the wood sliver, the piece of straw and the toy soldier. She had to get downstairs right now!

It was a busy day that Monday, and therefore it gave Jenny little opportunity to think about her continuing dream, but from time to time she caught herself drifting into deep thoughts about it. From the start, this manuscript had set the ground rules and it appeared that they were as such: One chapter at a time only. Her attempts to read ahead had resulted in none of the magic she had experienced when she followed the rules. Besides, the script only took her to the dream. It didn't replicate it in any form or fashion. Basically it wasn't even the same story when she re-read it.

The other mystery was she couldn't remember much about the dreams except the characters and some of the places she had appeared. Jenny remembered Garth as if he had been seared into her mind, and Josh to a lesser degree. She remembered the house and the graves, and a vague location in the state. For some reason World War I seemed to be implicated, but right now she couldn't make the connection. Something else that bothered her was the feeling that she was part of this story, and not just visiting it. The closeness with Garth and the bond with Josh, those didn't just happen, when she happened to appear on the scene. Why was she only being allowed to retain these little snippets?

She had gone from astonishment at what was happening, to a now grim determination to get to the bottom of the story. She would just have to play by the rules, and tonight would be no exception. She was not going to understand the dream until she got to the last chapter. An eerie feeling came over her. Where would she stay, there or here?

Caroline and Jenny were taking a break in the back of the store. The weather outside had gotten nasty and they had had no customers for the last hour or so. Oh, a few old ladies had stopped in to browse but that's all most of them did now was browse. Times where tough and not many people had money to spend on nonessentials.

"Have you ever had dreams you feel are trying to tell you a story?" Jenny asked her friend.

"Like what?" Caroline asked. "Oh Jennifer, are you dreaming about a man?" she added, giggling.

Jenny blushed and smiled. If Caroline only knew the man she had been dreaming about, but how could she tell her without looking like a complete fool?

She changed the subject. "Do you think we should have more fiction books or more books from local authors?" she asked.

Caroline was quiet for a moment. *There is a man. There is someone or something bothering her. Oh well, I mustn't pry. When she really wants to talk about it she will.*

"What kind of fiction books?" she asked.

Jenny had to work that evening because the two girls had finals and they needed the time to study. She remembered those days. In way she wished she was still in school. The pressure was nothing compared to the pressure she was under now.

She walked around the store straightening up and shutting off the lights. Business was slow so she would close a little early tonight. Beside's she had another date with a manuscript.

CHAPTER TEN

She ate her supper slowly and carefully, as if she was preparing her body for some great journey, and she had to be ready for it. Dishes done and everything put away, she went in the bathroom to prepare her bath. For a while today she had given some thought to skipping the bath and grabbing the manuscript and getting right to it. But then she thought of Garth, and she knew she was going to see him once more, and she wanted to look and smell her best.

She undressed and eased herself into the warm water. She added some scented bath salts and oil to the water and the whole room smelled nice. She washed carefully and then lounged in the water as if she was enjoying the bathtub for what could be a long time. It was just another feeling she couldn't explain.

Finally dried off and in a clean nightgown, Jenny brushed her hair and then adjusted the lamp. She picked up Chapter Six and held the pages steady. It was time.

It was springtime and the snow had gone from the farm but the weather still carried that hint of coolness. Maybe Mother Nature was not quiet ready to give in yet. Jennifer was on her knees in the garden and Garth was tilling and raking out the soil beside her. In her apron pocket were little bags of seeds that Garth had collected from last years crop and hung in the granary over the winter. Beans, corn, peas and a bucket of seed potatoes sat ready for her by the edge of the black soil. Garth worked quietly, humming to himself, and stopping from time to time to look her way and smile. Josh didn't appear to be around right now and she suddenly missed him but didn't question where he was.

The Magic Book

By late afternoon they had finished with what they could do for now, and they both retreated to the house with muddy hands and faces to clean up. Garth had put a copper boiler full of water on the kitchen stove before they came out, so it would be warm.

"I'll wait out here for you to wash," he said, as they approached the porch and sat down on the step.

Jenny, alone in the kitchen took off her dress, and standing in her petticoat proceeded to clean herself from the dirt and sweat. When she was finished she put on a clean dress and went outside and took her place on the step. She took a wire brush that hung on the wall and combed the burrs out of the old dog's hair. She could hear Garth still humming that same tune in the kitchen. She had heard it someplace before but didn't know where, but the words, "The Yanks are Coming," seemed to be part of it.

"Lets go for a walk," Garth said; back outside now and in a clean shirt. "I have something I want to tell you and this weather makes me want to be outside. This winter was way too long and beside's I have a new calf to show you, just born yesterday. The mother didn't come in with the others last night and when I went out in the pasture to look for her it had all ready happened."

Garth, Jennifer and the dog picked their waythrough the pasture, still wet and muddy from spring rains. The cows were all congregated under one tree and watched them approaching while lying down chewing their cuds. The mother cow turned as if to protect her calf that was nursing, but they all seemed comfortable with the intruders. After inspecting the cow and her calf, they walked down along the edge of a small creek, swollen over its banks from the snowmelt and sat down on a fallen log facing the water.

Garth put his arm around her and held her close to him. "Jennifer we've been together for some time now and I've grown very fond of you. For a long time I've wanted to ask you to be my wife. I wasn't sure if I would ever get married again after Priscilla died. Oh, I got over her's and the baby's death in time, but not being able to care for Josh, and having him go to live with his grandparents was hard on me. He really was all I had left. I knew if I did get married again it would have to be someone who would love Josh too. You seem to fill that void in both of us, but I realize now, that how you feel about us-- is so important here. How *do* you feel about us Jennifer?"

She had tears in her eyes when she turned to face him. "I love you both so much Garth, and yes, I would love to be your wife and Josh's mother."

They embraced and kissed passionately, but then Garth abruptly pulled away, saying, "There is one thing I must do before we get married my love. I have thought about this long and hard and there is no way I can get it out of my mind. I have to go fight in the war. President Wilson has asked all able-bodied men to respond to the war effort. It is my God given duty Jennifer, but as soon as the war is over and I come home, we'll get married. In the meantime I would like you to live here and take care of Josh and the farm. The neighbors will take care of the crops for you."

It was more like a business agreement than a proposal. She was stunned and had a rough time forming the words. "Why not get married right now Garth?"

"Because Jennifer if the unthinkable did happen, I don't want you to be a widow. I know how that feels and believe me, it's better this way."

"I believe you, but I don't understand," she said. "That should be my concern Garth, not yours."

They walked back to the house quietly hand in hand. It was starting to get dark. Finally back at the steps she asked. "When would you be going?"

"In a few days," he said quietly. "I have already signed up and received my training."

They went inside and she clung to him as if he was leaving in a few minutes instead of a few days. Their kisses were deeper than before, and flames of passion were lit in both of them. He picked her up and took her to his bedroom, a room she had never been in before. They kissed and their hands roamed to parts of their bodies that had seemed inappropriate until now. Slowly, and so careful that it was almost as if they were asking each other's permission before each move, before each touch, they undressed each other until they lay nude in each other's arms. She felt his passion and longing for her and although she had never been with a man, she knew the obvious signs. She felt, being one with Garth was the only way to satisfy an urging in her body that she was now experiencing, and she was ready to give herself to him now. Suddenly he stopped the petting and sat up.

"This too must wait my love," he said. If you were to get pregnant and left here alone with just Josh, it could be very dangerous. I need to be with you when our babies are born. Our day will come, as soon as the war is over. Then we will make love with no constraints and it will be so beautiful."

Jennifer was suddenly aware of her nakedness and took her dress and held it in front of her, covering herself. "I don't understand Garth. I don't understand any of this," she cried, "but I'll be here waiting for you, right here in this bed when you come home, and come home you better." Then she turned over and sobbed into the pillow.

Jenny was cold when she woke up. The covers were all on the floor. Chapter Six was on the side of the bed turned over, and she was naked. She had no questions this time about why. She knew why she was naked. She could feel the unfilled desire that was still within her. She put her nightgown back on and went to sleep, hugging her pillow to her body.

The next morning and throughout the day Jenny was unnaturally quiet, even to the point that Caroline asked her, "What's the matter, aren't you feeling well?"

"Oh nothing," she answered and smiled. "Just a few things on my mind that I have to sort out for myself."

She had retained more of the dream in her memory this time than before. In fact if she thought about it, with each chapter she remembered more than the previous one. Was that because the story was building on itself or was it trying to tell her something?

She was unsettled today, and she could feel sexual tension that had never been awakened in her young body before. Today for some reason that curiosity had been replaced with a fire that burned in her body and it was being fueled by thoughts of her and Garth naked on the bed in his house: The way he had touched her and caressed and kissed her, and the way she had been driven to wanting him to consummate their love right then and there. That was not at all like the Jennifer she knew.

Jenny was so confused right now. Maybe if she had ever had a normal relationship with a man in the past she would understand what was happening to her, but no, she had never allowed any of that in her carefully structured life.

Getting past the sexual tension, she thought about Garth and the war. *What was the message here? Had he had come home a hero and married her, or worse had he not come home at all? Had she lived on that farm in another life and all of this was just coming out of her subconscious mind like Bridey Murphy or whatever her damn name was who was hypnotized and told of her life in Ireland through the mouth of a woman in Colorado. It was all so frustrating.*

What about Josh? Had she raised him and if he was real, was he still alive. Garth would be dead or very old today by any stretch of the imagination. It was nineteen seventy-four and he would have to be ninty, but Josh was only four then.

The day dragged on and she busied herself with some things she had been putting off for while, anything to get away from that dream for a while. She did some dusting and rearranged some books on the shelves. She even worked until closing that night letting both of the college girls have the night off. It was close to ten before she finally closed the store and went upstairs to make her supper and get ready for bed.

CHAPTER ELEVEN

As Jenny lounged in the tub she was little apprehensive tonight. She knew that there were only two chapters left in the manuscript, and one thing she hadn't found out in her dream was Garth's last name. If something had happened to him she would be hard pressed to find out anything more about him without a family name. In fact if he had come home to her and Josh, she would still need that information to confirm the story. That is if she wanted to.

She caught herself fantasizing about her missing sexual connection with Garth. She still didn't understand why he hadn't married her. Most people would have wanted to cement that relationship before they left for war.

What would it have been like to actually consummate their relationship and be one with each other. To hold him as close as you can possibly hold anyone and know they were man and wife. Her thoughts drifted to that spring day in the bedroom when they had bared their bodies and their emotions. She could still feel his touch and smell his scent. At last, somewhat frustrated over her confusing thoughts, she pulled the plug and drained the water away. It was time to face the music.

In bed with the light adjusted, and warm and snug she picked up Chapter Seven.

She was sitting at the kitchen table in Garth's house, alone, but she had the sense that Josh was there someplace. In her hand was a letter. The first one she had received from Garth since he had boarded the train in his uniform that day in town. He had looked so handsome in his uniform and she had been so proud of him. She looked down at her hands as she held the brown envelope. Her nails were filled with dirt, and cracked, and broken from working in the garden. The hem of her dress was torn and her arms were tanned a deep brown. She swiped at the loose strands of hair that were always falling in her face. She needed to wash and clean up badly but there had been no time. Maybe after she read the letter.

The stationary inside was a light brown, to match the envelope. It began.

To my Darling Jennifer.

Today I am at the pier in New York waiting to board ship for England. From there it is anyone's guess where we are heading, but the word is out that our outfit will probably be sent to France to stop the German advance. I will let you know as soon as I can, but the mail from overseas is notoriously slow so you might be reading about things that happened a month ago. Today is May 1st.

New York is huge and such a bustling city. I was in St. Paul and Minneapolis a few times, but they are small compared to this. It's not just the war effort that has made it so busy; it is a very important commerce center.

How is Josh, and how are you getting along? I know I left you in a very difficult position and I feel bad about that. I hope the woodpile I left is enough to last you through the winter, if it comes to that. If not don't be afraid to ask the neighbors for help.

Well our ship is boarding right now so I do want to mail this before I leave the states. I wish for a quick end to the war. I wish for your arms and the arms of my son.-----Love Garth

Jennifer turned the envelope over and read the return address. It was just a military P.O. box.

Josh had been napping and it was time for the two of them to go milk the cows. Josh was no help, but she kept him close whenever she was doing chores. For a second the dream stalled, but then she was back with Josh and they were sitting on a wooden swing in the yard. He was lying with his head in her lap and she was singing softly to him. What a precious little boy he was, and what a good age to be, with his father gone. His long-term memory had not come into play much at times like this. A horse was coming up the drive and Jennifer stood and set the boy behind her. It was the neighbor, so she breathed a sigh of relief.

The Magic Book

"I was just in town," the man said without dismounting. "I took the liberty of picking up your mail. I know how hard it is for you to get away."

"Thank you," she said. "You've all been so very kind."

"If I was younger I would be right there beside Garth," he said.

There were two letters and the new Sears and Roebuck catalog. One letter was from Garth and one was for him, from the county.

Her hands were trembling as she opened the letter from Garth. She gave Josh the catalog to look at while she read.

My darling Jennifer,

I am not sure what week it is back there now, but it is the middle of June here in France. We are getting a few days to rest up before we go to a new location. We were in heavy combat with the Germans this past week at a place called Belleau Wood, and our division under Commander Jack Pershing pushed them back across the River Marne. It was not without heavy causalities however and I lost some good friends. I, however, came through without a scratch so praise the Lord for that.

The Germans have used a lot of mustard gas so we have to keep our gas masks ready at all times when we are in the trenches.

I imagine you are canning vegetables by now or getting ready to. How is Josh? I lie awake nights thinking about both of you and how nice it will be to be home again and for there to be peace in this world. Write when you can.

Love Garth

The dream now seemed to be in fast motion and she was only catching bits and pieces of it.

The neighbors were there cutting and bringing in the hay and at one point the kitchen table was filled with mason jars full of vegetables, jelly and jam. She had gone to church several times and went to the neighbors for supper a few times but they hadn't been to town in weeks. Maybe tomorrow she would hitch up the horse and they would ride in.

The ride to town the next day was long and Josh grew restless and she had to stop a few times to let him get out and stretch his legs. She went to the general store and bought flour and salt. She also bought some spices and a few yards of material. It was cotton and she wanted to make some clothes for Josh. He was growing so fast this summer.

On the way out of town she stopped at the post office. Yes, there was a letter for her, and it had just come today.

From the moment she opened the letter sitting in the carriage in front of the post office she knew something bad had happened and her hand went to her face to hide her concern from the passerby's. It began:

Dear Jennifer,

You don't know me but I am a friend of Garths and he has asked me to write to you for him. I don't want to worry you too much, but Garth was injured in a battle last week on the western front. He was picked up last night by medics and he will be transferred either to England or a hospital ship to go home. I am sure Garth will not be able to stay in the war effort. In either case the war department should be notifying you soon as to his whereabouts and condition.

Sincerely yours, Clayton Wilson.

Jennifer jumped down, untied the horse, climbed back aboard and cracked the reins, and they took off down the street and out of town. She could hardly see through her tears, and now the first sob chocked from her throat and she gathered Josh to her side as he was crying too, even though had no idea why.

When she awoke her face was wet with tears. She sat up and blew her nose. Once more she remembered much more than before, including the letters. But the one big mystery she still hadn't solved. Garths last name. *She had to know it*, she reasoned. *He had written her letters and she had written him. For Gods sake, she had lived in his house and taken care of his child and the farm. It had to have been revealed to her someplace. Why was she not allowed to see it?*

She did understand one thing though. The dream was only letting her see what it wanted her to see. Only letting her remember what it wanted her to remember. She put Chapter Seven on top of the others. She had no idea what Chapter Eight was going to say. Just fears about what it might, or might not say. It was only a couple of pages long, but It would have to wait for tomorrow. That seemed to be the unwritten rule.

Jenny was troubled now and going back to sleep seemed to be almost impossible. She got up and made some coffee and watched television until the station signed off the air. Back in bed, she lay for another hour just thinking, until she finally drifted off to sleep. The next day she was tired and somewhat disoriented from too little sleep and too much worry. Caroline, again concerned, asked Jenny how she was and remarked on her lackluster attitude, but Jenny just shrugged it off. She wanted to tell her; I have this manuscript I've been reading that is driving me out of my damn mind, and there is this man in the story who I've fallen in love with but he doesn't exist anywhere but in my screwed up state of mind, so that my friend is why I am in such a pissy mood, so there, but she didn't.

She just tried to avoid people as much as she could. Maybe tomorrow everything would be explained and everything would be fine again. Just maybe she could go on with her life again.

That night when Caroline had her coat on to go home Jenny told her, "I'm sorry for being so out of sorts. I got my period today and I just feel awful. I know that's no reason to treat you or anyone badly."

Caroline laughed and gave her one of those little half hugs. "Well I know one good way to stop those periods girl, and I don't mean menopause, but the down side of it is the little imps take forever to grow up."

Jenny laughingly replied, "Someday---maybe---who knows? Good night Caroline."

After Caroline left she thought to herself. *That's one good thing about being a girl. You can always blame everything on your period, and no one is going to check to see if you're telling the truth or not.* She laughed at the thought.

When the day was over and she faced the prospect of reading the last chapter, it was not without some trepidation. She knew the end of the story meant the end of Garth, and the end of Garth meant the end of the only love affair she had ever experienced. It was going to be sad, no matter how the story turned out.

She spent more time in the tub then on other nights trying to get up the fortitude to face her fate, but at last she dried off, put on her nightgown and went and sat on the edge of the bed. The manuscript sat in two stacks. The finished pile was turned over and about a half inch thick. Chapter Eight was staring her in the face so she picked it up. It was just a few pages.

CHAPTER TWELVE

She had been canning pickles that day when the drab green motorized military truck came nosily down the lane. She had heard it long before she recognized it as a government vehicle, and watched it bouncing over the ruts and holes in the sandy road. Now she stood shading her eyes from the setting sun and when it turned toward the house her heart started racing. Was Garth coming home?

The car stopped and two men in Army uniforms got out, but neither one of them was Garth, and then somehow she knew the news was not going to be good. She peered back toward the vehicle looking for someone else, but it appeared to be empty. The shorter of the two men approached her while the other stayed a few steps behind.

"Are you Jennifer, the fiancé of Garth Gildabran?"

For a second her voice didn't work, but finally a little squeak came out that said, "Yes."

"Miss, I regret to inform you that Garth Gildabran was injured in combat in France. He was transformed to a hospital ship and sent to New York for treatment, but he passed away before the ship could dock. I have this for you." He handed her a Western Union telegram that said essentially what he had just told her.

Jennifer read it slowly and deliberately. Then still not showing any emotion she asked, "Where is his body?"

This time the taller man spoke up while he nervously fingered his hat. "It's on the train to St. James right now. It should arrive tomorrow. The body has been prepared for burial and will be accompanied by two soldiers. However, it will be your responsibility, or the family's, to have someone pick it up and take it to its final resting place." They both expressed their condolences got back in the car and left.

She watched the car disappear into the setting sun, her head held high. Then slowly her hands began to shake and she fell to her knees sobbing.

Jennifer wept for over an hour, and then slowly she realized it was starting to get dark and she needed help. She went into the house and looked down at Josh who had been sleeping the whole time. She dressed him and he walked outside with her, rubbing his eyes, seemingly confused at what he was doing out here at bedtime. She hitched up Josie and then they proceeded down the lane to the road in the dark. They turned left and headed up the road to the small white church.

When they got to the church it was dark, but she knew the Pastor lived right next door and there was a light on in his house. For a moment she sat in front of the house thinking about all the things she had to do. She had to arrange a funeral and she had to get someone with a wagon to go with her to St. James to retrieve Garths body. Then there was a grave to be dug and family to be notified. She walked slowly to the house, but the vicar had heard her horse and carriage and he met her outside.

"Reverend," she began. "I have some bad news and need your help. Garth has been killed in the war." She handed him the telegram still wet from her tears.

The old man read it carefully and then putting his arm around her said, "Come inside my child."

The pastor's wife made coffee and set out some bread and jam, but Jenny couldn't eat. She sipped the coffee slowly as the pastor talked, while Josh dozed on her lap.

"I will make the notification to the proper people," he said. "I will also accompany you to St. James in the morning to pick up, Garths body. We have men in the parish that will dig the grave. I am assuming he will be buried next to his wife and daughter."

"Yes," she said.

"Jennifer, Garth was a good man and the world will miss out on all of the things he would have accomplished, had he lived, but it will always be a better world for him having lived in it. I am so sorry."

He promised to be over first thing in the morning to pick her and Josh up and go to St. James. She thanked him and went out to the

The Magic Book

carriage. Even Josie looked sad in her harnesses with her head hung low. Somehow Jennifer felt the horse knew what was happening.

Sitting on the edge of the bed, she cradled Josh in her arms and rocked him slowly. Once he fell asleep she lay down beside him and cried herself to sleep, her nose buried in his curly locks.

Jennifer knew the next day that she would have to be strong, so when the pastor showed up she had somehow drawn on some courage from down deep inside of her. Josh remained in deep thought but under emotional control. She wasn't sure he really understood what had happened. The minister had borrowed a parishioner's truck and so the whole thing was a going to be a new experience for both of them riding in a gasoline powered vehicle. The very thing Garth had wished for. It was somewhat ironic.

They waited at the depot for about an hour and then the train pulled slowly into the station, and came to a stop with a huge hiss of steam and squealing brakes. The baggage car was right behind the engine and the coal tender, and as soon as the train stopped the big doors slid open, and there sat the coffin, covered with an American Flag. Two Honor Guards stood, one on each side of the casket.

A man from the station positioned a large green cart with red wheels up to the door and the casket was slid onto the wagon. Both of the Honor Guards, frozen at attention, snapped their hand to their caps in a final salute to their fallen comrade in the casket, and then the big door slammed shut. There was another blast of steam from the engine and the train lurched forward, slowly picking up speed and was soon gone from sight around the bend.

Jennifer and Josh stood and watched as the casket was transferred from the wagon to the back of the truck and lashed in place. It was time to take Garth home.

The ride back was quiet. Josh kept looking back over the seat at the box in the back, but he didn't ask any questions.

Jennifer talked quietly with the Reverend while he tried to comfort her with biblical passages and words. She remained mostly stoic and unmoved. She had gone past the grief stage for the moment, and could only think that half a world away people were still killing each other. Most of them had no idea why, except to say it was for their country. Somewhere out there was another man still alive that had taken the life of the only man she ever loved and had made his son an orphan, and for that reason, right now she hated him.

It was dark when they got home and the Vicar told Jennifer he would have the funeral service at eleven the next morning. "Do you want to leave Garth's body on the truck, or should I leave it with you?" he asked.

"Please leave it on the porch," she said.

All night long she maintained a lonely vigil sitting on a kitchen chair wrapped in a blanket overlooking the flag draped casket, with a lantern burning next to it. She knew it was sealed and she would not be allowed to see his dead face or kiss it. She had seen it for the last time the day he left.

At daybreak she went inside and put on her black dress and bonnet. She would have to get Josh up in an hour or so. She walked to the gravesite and saw the freshly laid back dirt and flowers that had been put in place. They had dug the grave yesterday while she was gone. If there was any consoling message from this grave, it could only be that he was back with the first woman he loved, and his child. He had loved Jennifer too, but she had never really been his. Only betrothed.

She walked around the rest of the property recalling the first day she met him in the hay field. She remembered the day at the fair and the holidays they spent together, and the time they had lay naked together on Garths bed and professed their love but didn't consummate it. She walked to the stable and petted the noses of Josie and Adam. They were always standing together. They had to know what love was.

She walked behind the barn and looked out over the empty pasture. She remembered the day she and Garth had sat by the creek and talked. Maybe that was the first time she actually felt he loved her too. It was time to get Josh up.

Two boys came a few minutes later and did her chores in the barn. She didn't speak to them; she just watched them from the kitchen window. Not long after buggies, carriages, and automobiles flooded the yard. So many people she could hardly count them all. They unloaded tables and chairs and women spread tablecloths and filled them with food and drink. Many of them came inside to express their condolences. Josh's grandparents arrived and took him under their wing.

It was time for the funeral and Jennifer sat huddled with Josh's grandparents in front of the grave. The old pastor talked softly and kindly about Garth and his life. His eulogy was comforting to all. Then it was time to lower the coffin and four men came to handle the ropes. As soon as they were done, Jennifer stood and picked up a hand-full of soil and sprinkled it on top of the box. The flag was presented to Josh's grandparents and the crowd walked back to the lunch tables.

The rest of the day was just a blur of activity, but one by one they left. The grave had been covered over and Jennifer went into the house, alone again with her thoughts. Josh had gone home with his grandparents. Exhausted she laid her head down on the kitchen table and fell asleep.

When Jenny woke up she was sad, but somehow still fulfilled. She now knew what had happened to Garth and somehow she had come to the realization that she had been afforded this special look into the past. That Garth had come to her and showed her what it was to love a man. What is was to have a family and a home. Garth had to die because this was not reality, but he showed her the way to reality.

She did have a couple of questions, however, and the first was answered when she took the box and carefully turned the manuscript back over to the first page. G. J. Gildabran was Garth Gildabran and he had written this story. *But what about the last chapter, she wondered. He couldn't write his own epitaph. Who wrote Chapter Eight?* Jenny dug through the pages once more until she came to the first page of Chapter Eight. Something was different this time as she reread the last chapter. The words mirrored the story, and she remembered all of it. The rest of the manuscript had not been that way. Then she noticed the penmanship was different. Why had she not noticed that before? Jenny paged through to the last page, the last line, and there it was. Faintly as if it had been added in pencil.

This story was finished by Jennifer. September 9th, 1918

Jenny was crying now and holding the manuscript to her bosom. This was not just Garths story it was her story too.

CHAPTER THIRTEEN

The next few weeks went by slowly as Jenny tried to get on with her life and tried to put away what had happened so many years ago. She put the manuscript away, vowing to never look at it again.

The store was getting more prosperous as the days went by, and before she realized it, spring had come to St. Paul once again. She loved to walk down by the river and sit in the park not far from her house. She began to notice men more than she had in the past and although nothing serious had come along, she had had some dates with men she met socially, and through the library board where she was now a member. Life seemed good.

In late May, not able to forget the dream-- but able to live with it-- she decided to take a trip to St. James after visiting her fathers grave on Memorial Day. When she went to his grave, the feeling of loneliness came flooding back, and she cried softly as she put flowers by his headstone. Her life had been so busy she hadn't had much time to think about her dad. After a few minutes Jenny thought about another grave a long way away. It was early in the day and surely she had the time to go and try to find it. Why not, she thought, maybe it would give her some closure.

The ride down to St. James was about two hours, and she tired to formulate a plan once she got there. How was she going to find the place?

The sleepy little town was nearly deserted when she arrived and very few places of business were open. Jenny did find a convenience store open so she stopped and filled the car with gas. The man behind the checkout register looked bored reading a paper and drinking coffee.

"That be it?" he asked as he rang up her gas.

The Magic Book

"Yes, but can I ask you a question. Have you lived here long?"

"Most of my life," he said. "What is it you want to know?" He seemed enthusiastic just to have someone to talk to.

"Does the name Gildabran come to mind?"

The man thought for a second and said. "Not right of the top of my head but it is familiar. Just a second," he said, and got out the phone book.

He hummed some nondescript song as he paged through the book finally stomping his finger down on a page. "There are two Gildabran's in here. One lives here in town and one lives out in the country a few miles. I do know the one in town come to think of it. He's an Attorney. He pushed the book towards her and Jenny looked at the page and the spot where his finger was pointing at an at.

Garth J. Gildabran, Attorney at Law. Specializing in wills and probate.

Jenny took the book from him and went back to the white pages in the front and looked up the name once more. There were two Gildabran names, Garth once more and Josh Gildabran, with a rural route address and a phone number. Jenny's heart was pounding.

"Are you alright?" the man asked.

She didn't answer his question but followed it up with one of her own. "Who can tell me how to get there?" she asked and pointed to Josh's address.

He swung the book back around and looked carefully at the address. "I can," he said.

Armed with directions Jenny drove west out of town on a tar, but rural road. The landscaped was dotted with farms and rolling hills. The world was a carpet of green and she could smell the fresh scent of alfalfa and sweet clover as she drove by the fields. The corn was just starting to poke out of the rich black soil.

At an intersection about four miles from town she had been instructed to turn left on a gravel road. "The house should be about a mile up on the left," he had said. She drove slowly looking for anything that she might remember from her dreams, but realizing that it had been over fifty years since she had last seen it, and then only in it's mystic form.

It was the hay field by the road that she recognized and coasted to stop. It was still a hay field and suddenly the memory of that day when she had first appeared here, came rushing back to her; When Garth had been picking up hay in the field with the horses. She remembered very little from that first encounter but she did remember one thing he had said. "You are where you belong." She didn't know then what he had meant, but she knew now.

Looking behind her and to her left she saw an old house but it didn't look like the one she remembered. Was it the same place? There were no other buildings except a modern garage. Jenny backed up and went into the driveway and stopped. What would she say to the people? She read the name on the mailbox. It said Josh Gildabran. She was sweating and ran her handkerchief across her forehead. This was crazy and they would think she was crazy if she tried to explain.

Then slowly she put the car in gear and drove up to the house. If they were home, she would just show them the manuscript. It sat beside her on the other seat.

Jenny walked up to the back door of the house, her heart in her throat. She had been here before, she could just feel it. She reached up and knocked on the door. From inside a dog barked, but no one came, so she knocked again, but still only the dog.

She stood on the step for a few seconds thinking about what she should do. Just leave, was her first impulse, but then something drew her attention across the yard. It was a tombstone, and there were fresh flowers next to it. She walked slowly toward it, not wiling herself to do so but being drawn toward it by some inexplicable force. It was a fairly new stone and it simply said Gildabran across the top. Underneath in small letters it said Garth J-- August 12th 1918 and Priscilla C & infant June 1st, 1912. No birth dates. Jenny was crying now and then she remembered the flowers she had brought in the car just in case, and she went and got them. She retuned to the grave and dug out some soil with her bare hands and planted the geraniums next to the existing ones.

Try as she may she couldn't remember much about Garth. It wasn't even close to what she had remembered in her dreams. She did mediate for few minutes however. That is until--until she heard the car in the driveway.

The Magic Book

Jenny walked a little ways away from the grave. She was not looking forward to any confrontation, and right now she had no idea what she was going to say. The car stopped and two men got out. Both of them were staring at her. The older man stayed by the car but the younger one came toward her. He was just a few feet away from her when he spoke, but not before he obviously saw what she had done at the grave.

"Who are you, and what are you doing here?" he asked, with a puzzled look on his face.

"My name is Jennifer Crawford," she said extending her hand.

He took it loosely.

I think I have something you will be interested in, that may help explain why I'm here." She indicated that she had to go to her car. She reached in and retrieved the box and approached both men who were now standing side by side.

Turning to the older man, she asked, "Are you Josh?"

"Yes," he answered. "How did you know that?"

Jenny didn't answer his question but reached in the box and brought out the manuscript. "I believe this was your fathers," she said. "He was Garth, right?"

The man looked astonished, but he took the stack of papers and stared at them. She had given it to him with the first page, with his Dads signature, showing right on top.

He looked at Jenny and then he looked back at the papers and then back to her again. "Are you saying my father wrote this?" he asked.

"I'm going to leave it for you. Both of you read it and then you tell me. Here's my card." Jenny gave them her business card that simply said. 'Jenny's Books.' It gave her address and phone number.

Garth looked at her and said, "Can I ask you where you found it?"

"I bought an old book store and it was in a box with some papers."

"How did you find us, and why the flowers?" He nodded toward the grave.

"Read it, and then I think you will understand," Jenny said. "I have to go."

Jenny drove back to St. Paul and never had she been more proud of herself for having the intestinal fortitude to do what she had done today. It was as if a great weight had been lifted from her mind and now she could go on with the business of running her bookstore, and getting on with her life.

As for Garth, he had in this mysterious way given her a touch of life and love she never could have received any other way. She planed to come out of her shell and look for love and happiness.

It was the middle of June, on one fine summer day when Jenny went to have coffee with an old friend in the back of the store, and left Caroline up front. A few minutes later Caroline came back and told her that there was young man who wanted to talk with her.

"Did he say who he was?" Jenny asked. A little perturbed at being interrupted in her conversation.

"No," Caroline said, "but he did say you would want to talk with him."

She excused herself and walked up to meet him. He was looking at a book with his back towards her. When he turned to meet her, Jenny instantly recognized him.

"Remember me?" he asked.

"Yes, of course I do. How are you Garth?"

"I'm fine," he said. 'Jenny, Dad and I did some research and the manuscript that you gave us was written by my Grandfather, and it does appear to be authentic. I was amazed, when reading it, how the story brought you to us. I didn't find the correlation. You must have been a better reader than we were."

"Maybe I saw it in different way than you did," she said. "I'm just glad to get it back to you."

"Yes, it made my father very happy," Garth said.

"Can I ask you who you thought wrote the last chapter? I was not able to find any name and Grandpa could not have written about his own demise."

"That was strange wasn't it?"

They talked for a few more minutes and then Garth said," I won't keep you any longer I just wanted to stop by and say thank you."

"Your welcome," She replied.

Garth shook her hand and started for the door but then stopped and turning said to Jenny. "I like your store, do you run it by yourself?"

"Yes, but I do have some hired help. I'm not married." For a second she wondered why she had said that.

Garth smiled. "I'm not married either. Would you like to have coffee or a drink sometime?"

"I would love that," she said.

Mike Holst